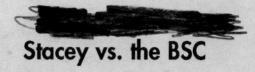

Stacey vs. the BSC

Stacey vs. the BSC

AN
APPLE
PAPERBACK

SCHOLASTIC INC.
New York Toronto London Auckland Sydney

For Molly Sumner
and everyone in
Wauwatosa, WI

*The author gratefully acknowledges
Peter Lerangis
for his help in
preparing this manuscript.*

Cover art by Hodges Soileau

ISBN 0-590-48235-1

12 11 10 9 8 7 6 5 4 3 2 1   4 5 6 7 8 9/9 0/0

Printed in the U.S.A.   40

First Scholastic printing, March 1995

*C*_{runch}.

Claudia Kishi was eating something sweet and chocolatey. I couldn't tell what it was, but I sure could smell it.

"Just hold it a few more minutes, Stacey," she said, peeking around her easel.

I swallowed. That was about all I was allowed to do. That, and blink. If I stretched, talked, even nodded, Claudia would have a cow.

Being an artist's model isn't easy. Especially the way Claudia had posed me. I was staring off into space with a dreamy, thoughtful expression, leaning on one elbow.

My back was killing me.

What was worse, my nose had started to itch. I crinkled it, but that made the itch worse. Then I shook my head quickly.

"Uh-uh-*uhhh*," Claud warned me.

I held my breath. I tried to imagine a finger

scratching my nose. I forced myself to think of something else. A tropical beach . . . a sunrise . . . a breeze . . . wafting gently . . . right up my nose. . . .

"Ahhh —"

"Not now, Stacey!" Claudia cried.

"*Ahhh* —"

"No! Hold it in!"

"*CHOOOO!*"

Too late. My hair went flying into my face. My elbow slipped off the armrest. I sent a spray across Claudia's night table.

I looked at Claudia. She was staring at the table. Her jaw was wide open (which, believe me, was not *too* attractive). I gulped.

"*Très* elegant, McGill," Claudia said.

I tried to hold back a giggle. I was just about to apologize when Claudia lost it. She burst out laughing so hard, she dropped her paintbrush.

Me? I howled.

The two of us sounded like hyenas. We could not stop. The door to Claudia's room swung open and her sister, Janine the Genius, peeked in.

She shook her head. "Uh, would you mind lowering the volume a bit?"

"Sorry," Claud and I both said.

Janine wandered over to Claudia's painting

2

and peered at it. "Very, um, creative," she said.

Uh-oh.

I didn't like the sound of that remark.

As Janine left, I peeked around Claudia's easel.

Her painting was . . . colorful.

In fact, it was big splotches of colors. All over the canvas. With no resemblance to a human face.

"You hate it," Claudia said.

"No! I mean, it's gorgeous, but I guess . . . I'm not sure why I had to hold that pose." I sighed. "It just doesn't look like *me*, Claud."

"It's a suggestion of you, Stace," Claudia explained. "You know, like your essence. That's why I used all the golden colors over here. See? And the piercing blue here."

My hair was a yellow swirl, my eyes were blue glops, and my clothes were a multicolor smear.

But I had to admit, it looked cool. Hey, I've seen abstract art before. I grew up in New York City, and my parents took me to plenty of museums and art galleries.

Not to mention phenomenal restaurants and boutiques and theaters and festivals.

Sigh. Do I sound as if I miss the Big Apple?

I do, sometimes. But I get to visit a lot, because my dad still lives there.

I guess I'm lucky, although it's hard to think of yourself as lucky after your parents divorce. The divorce is the reason Mom and I moved here, to Stoneybrook, Connecticut.

Or I should say, moved *back* to Stoneybrook. The first time was BD (Before the Divorce), when Dad's company made him relocate to Connecticut. We'd barely settled in when the company made Dad move back to the Big Apple again. All this moving, and a lot of other things, began wearing my parents down. Suddenly BD gave way to a big, ugly D. Mom wanted to move back to Stoneybrook, Dad wanted to stay in New York — and I was given a choice. What did I, Stacey McGill, the Ultimate Urbanite, do?

I went with Mom. Why? Because I'd grown to love Stoneybrook. I'd made some pretty cool friends (such as Claudia), and I'd joined the Baby-sitters Club, which, at the time, was about the most important thing in my life. (I'll tell you about the BSC later.)

Okay, so I don't see paintings in the Museum of Modern Art as often as I used to. Instead, I pose for a future famous artist. (Talk about talent. Claud can also draw, make jewelry, and sculpt.)

"I don't know." Claudia unwrapped a

Twinkie as she squinted at her painting. "I think it needs a little more oomphleesh."

Claudia is very chic, but she does have a habit of talking with her mouth full. What's *oomphleesh*? I didn't bother asking.

Honestly, I don't understand why Claudia does not look like the Goodyear Blimp. She *lives* on junk food. You should see her room. It's a dentist's nightmare — boxes of Goobers under the pillow, pretzels in the shoe rack, Mallomars on the hat shelf. Everything is hidden because Mr. and Mrs. Kishi are strict about Proper Eating. (Proper Reading, too. Claudia even has to hide her Nancy Drew books, believe it or not.)

Anyway, Claudia the Chocoholic is thin, blemish-free, and stunning. She's Japanese-American, with gorgeous jet-black hair and almond-shaped eyes. And her outfits are as abstract as her paintings. That day, for example, she was wearing this super-baggy man's shirt that must have once belonged to a sumo wrestler, enormous light wool black trousers gathered at the waist with a silken sash, and old work boots. Her hair was pulled back with a barrette in the shape of a set of teeth. Very original, very cool.

Me? I'm just as clothes-conscious as Claudia. But my style is less funky. I like sophisticated, up-to-the-minute fashions.

That's not the only way Claud and I are different. For one thing, I have blonde hair and blue eyes. For another, I cannot eat junk food. Literally. You see, I'm a diabetic. For me, sugary foods are like poison. My body can't regulate blood sugar, so I have to inject myself with a hormone called insulin every day. I know, it sounds gross, but believe me, you get used to it.

Claudia broke into a big smile and painted a purple arc over the top right corner of the canvas. "That's *it!*" she cried. "That's what I needed. You know, for balance!"

Uh-huh. Sure. "Beautiful," I said.

"Want some?" Claudia held out an open bag of sesame-seed pretzels (which I can eat).

"No, thanks," I said. "I'm going out to dinner with Robert tonight. I need to leave room." (Robert Brewster is my boyfriend.)

"Where are you two going?" Claudia asked.

"To the Rosebud Cafe and then the cineplex," I said. "He wants to see this basketball movie —"

"Oh, gag me. The new Jason Priestley movie's playing there, too. Very hot. Definitely skip the basketball. You can convince him."

That's another thing I like about Claudia. She has a cool attitude about guys. Around her, I can talk about Robert and she won't giggle or act weird.

You know what had happened when I'd mentioned my date at the Friday BSC meeting? Kristy Thomas (our president) started singing, "Stacey and Robert, sitting in a tree, K-I-S-S-I-N-G!" Okay, it was a joke, but I mean, we *are* in eighth grade.

Dawn Schafer, another club member, told Kristy the song was dumb. And Claudia rolled her eyes. But all the others thought it was the funniest thing.

See what I have to put up with for LUV?

Now, don't get me wrong. I adore my Baby-sitters Club friends. They have zillions of great qualities. And some of them even have boyfriends of their own. Kristy, for instance, goes out with a guy named Bart Taylor. (Although that's kind of a sports romance. Their idea of a hot date is batting practice.) Even our shyest member, Mary Anne Spier, has a steady guy — as does Mallory Pike (sort of), one of our two sixth-grade members. (The rest of us are thirteen-year-old eighth-graders.)

So why do they act so strange about boys? It's just a wavelength thing, I think. Take Claudia. Even though she doesn't have anyone steady, she and I are definitely on the same wavelength about guys.

"Anastasia . . ." Claudia said softly.

I gave Claudia a Look. She never calls me by my full name.

". . . *Fantasia*," she continued. "That's what I'll call the painting — *Anastasia Fantasia*."

"Great idea," I said. Even though I thought it sounded like the name of a cartoon.

We hung out awhile longer. Claudia put the painting against the wall to dry. Janine came in again and asked if Claud's painting was a still life or a landscape. (Grrr.)

Afterward I walked to Robert's. It was a clear, chilly March evening. The trees were bare and gray-looking, and patches of snow still clung to the curbs.

I was feeling happy and calm until I turned onto Robert's street.

Then it began. The Dance of the Empty Stomach. It happened every time at that same corner. My insides decided to do a little kick line, just to annoy me.

I guess I still didn't know him that well. Not that we'd just met or anything. We'd even spent some time together on Fire Island the summer before, but that had been complicated. My dad was there with his new girlfriend, and I had also invited Claudia along. Anyway, Robert and I had been going out as often as we could here in Stoneybrook. It's just that being in the Baby-sitters Club is a pretty big commitment. Your jobs have to come before your social life.

Okay, to be fair, I wasn't *that* nervous. I

mean, Robert is not exactly Mr. Intimidation. He's tall and handsome and thoughtful, and he has the cutest dimple on his left cheek when he smiles (which is often).

As I approached his house, I could see him sitting on his porch, talking with Wayne McConville. They were both wearing open windbreakers — in March! Just looking at them made me shiver.

They stood up when they saw me. Robert smiled and waved. My kick line took a quick bow and disappeared.

"Hi!" I called out, running across the lawn. "Aren't you cold?"

"Wayne and I were just shooting baskets," Robert replied.

"Don't worry," Wayne said with a grin. "I'm leaving."

Did I tell you Robert is an awesome athlete? He is. When I met him, he was on the Stoneybrook Middle School basketball team, and I was trying out for the cheerleading squad. Boy, did that experience open our eyes. We both realized the cheerleaders and athletes were treated like gods in our school — by students *and* teachers. It was so unfair to the other kids. Robert actually quit the team because of that, even though basketball was incredibly important to him. A lot of his teammates wouldn't speak to him afterward, but Robert stuck by his beliefs. (That's another thing. He's an independent thinker.)

All right, he's perfect. What can I say?

" 'Bye, you guys. Don't do anything I wouldn't do," Wayne called out as he started jogging home.

At least I think he said that. At that point, Robert and I were linking arms and smiling at each other.

"Are you going to change?" I asked, looking at his windbreaker.

His smile disappeared and he gave me this sad, droopy look. "I thought you liked me the way I am."

"No! I didn't mean *that* kind of change. I meant —"

Robert laughed. "Rank!" he said.

"Arrrrgh!" I gave him a playful shove, just as his mom walked into the living room.

"Ahem," she said, raising an eyebrow. "Beating up my fragile son?"

"Oops," I replied. Robert burst out laughing.

We piled into the car and chatted all the way to the Rosebud.

The meal? The movie? They were fine, but it didn't matter. I could have been in the desert and I would still have had a perfect evening.

CHAPTER 2

"Harrumph!" said Kristy Thomas. Her eyebrows arched way up as she looked at Claudia's clock.

Five thirty-seven.

Groan.

I was seven minutes late to the Baby-sitters Club's Monday meeting. This was my third or fourth lateness this month. Which sure didn't put me on Kristy's good side. She has this thing about punctuality. But this time I wasn't too worried. I had a good excuse.

"Sorry!" I said, catching my breath. "My bike blew a flat and I fell and twisted my ankle and by the time we made it back to my house I had to change — well, you know . . ." I limped into the room, taking off my coat.

"Are you okay?" Mary Anne Spier asked.

"Yeah." I flung the coat onto the floor and sat on Claudia's bed. "It's just a mild sprain."

"*We?*" Kristy said.

11

"Huh?" I asked.

"You said 'By the time *we* got home,' " Kristy replied.

"Yeah. Robert and me."

"Oh."

Kristy nodded. She and Mary Anne gave each other a quick glance. No one said a word.

Gulp.

"We rode to Mercer along the old road," I explained. "We would have been back much earlier if it weren't for the tire."

I was telling the truth. I'd had an accident. It wasn't my fault. But still, I felt so guilty.

So I shut up.

"Um, are you forgetting something?" Kristy asked.

I must have had *Duh* written all over my face. Then it dawned on me: "Oh!" I blurted out. "Dues day!"

Every Monday we all pay dues out of our earnings. As BSC treasurer, I collect the money. We use the money to help Claudia with her phone bill (her private line is the official BSC phone). We also have to buy supplies for Kid-Kits (small boxes of hand-me-down toys and activities we often take on our jobs), and to pay for events we dream up for the kids.

I reached in my backpack and took out a big manila envelope. Claudia, Kristy, Mary Anne,

Dawn, Jessica Ramsey, and Mallory Pike slooooowly searched for their money, grumbling and complaining.

Paying dues is not exactly a festive occasion at BSC meetings. But it's necessary. And whenever enough money is left over in the treasury, we use it for "discretionary surplus enhancement." Translation: pizza party! (Which no one complains about.)

The Baby-sitters Club, in case you hadn't noticed, is highly organized. Each member has a title, and most of us have official duties. We meet three times a week — Mondays, Wednesdays, and Fridays, from five-thirty to six o'clock — and we take phone calls from parents who need sitters. With seven members (nine, if you count our associates), we can cover just about all requests. That makes us *very* popular; our clients get one-stop shopping (one-call shopping?).

What genius thought of this brilliant idea? Why, *me*, thank you, thank you.

I wish.

No, the Baby-sitters Club sprang from the Amazing Mind of Kristy Thomas. It happened one fateful evening when she was in seventh grade. Her single, overworked mom was desperate for a sitter. She called and called but couldn't find anyone. So Kristy's Mind went into warp speed and the BSC was born. No more baby-sitting crises for Mrs. Thomas.

Actually, she's not Mrs. Thomas anymore. She married Watson Brewer, this mild-mannered millionaire who lives in a mansion in Stoneybrook's posh neighborhood. Kristy lives there now, with her three brothers (Charlie's seventeen, Sam's fifteen, and David Michael's seven); her adopted sister, Emily Michelle (who's from Vietnam); her grandmother, Nannie; two stepsiblings from Watson's previous marriage, Karen and Andrew Brewer, who are there every other month; and several pets. (By the way, don't ever talk to Kristy about her dad. He ran out on the family when Kristy was little, and she's bitter about it.)

If you walked into a BSC meeting, you'd know Kristy right away. She's the shortest, and she's usually dressed in jeans and sneakers — maybe cords, if she's feeling formal. She has medium brown hair, which she lets hang plainly. And she's the one with the big mouth. (I love her dearly, but she can be bossy.)

"Okay, pay up, come on," Kristy urged. "We have other club business to attend to."

Claudia started giggling. "Uh, what other business, Kristy?"

"Well . . . I haven't *called* for new business, so I don't *know* yet," Kristy said, turning red.

14

"You know the rules. I mean, it's a *meeting*."

Kristy huffed and puffed a little to herself as I finished collecting. "Okay, go ahead, Kristy," Claudia said.

Kristy cleared her throat. "Uh, ahem. Are there any items for discussion on the agenda?"

Everyone was trying not to crack up. Even Kristy.

Rrring! jangled the Official Phone.

Claudia snatched up the receiver. "Good afternoon, Baby-sitters Club. Oh, hi, Dr. Johanssen."

Jessica Ramsey and Mallory Pike started giggling and covering their mouths. I hoped Dr. Johanssen didn't hear them. They sounded like babies.

"What's so funny?" I whispered.

" '*Good afternoon*'?" Mal said, breaking into tee-hees.

Claudia usually greets people with a *hello*. I guess Mal and Jessi found the words *Good afternoon* hilarious. (They're the sixth-graders.)

"Thursday at four?" Claudia continued. "Just a minute." She looked at Mary Anne, who was flipping through the pages of the club record book.

"Um . . . Stacey's free," Mary Anne reported. (In the BSC, we don't usually "reserve" our charges, but Charlotte Johanssen is an exception. She and I are very close.)

Claud looked at me with a smile. "Anastasia?"

Jessi and Mal started tittering again. (This was beginning to bother me.)

"Sure," I said.

Robert and I had talked about taking another bike ride that day. But we hadn't made *definite* plans. Oh, well. A job is a job.

As Claudia talked to Dr. Johanssen, Mary Anne meticulously logged my job in the record book. Mary Anne is the BSC secretary, which is the hardest office, in my opinion. She records every sitting date, marks down all our many conflicts in advance (lessons, after-school activities, doctors' appointments), tries to make sure we all get a roughly equal amount of work, updates our client list, and keeps track of the rate each client pays.

It's enough to drive anyone else crazy. But not Mary Anne. She does it all calmly and happily, as if it were the easiest thing in the world. *Organized* is one of the first words that pops to mind with Mary Anne. Right alongside *quiet, sweet*, and *sensitive*. Super-sensitive. She sobs watching Barney. All you have to do is mention the words *Gone With the Wind* and her eyes well up.

Can you guess who Mary Anne the Meek's best friend is? Kristy the Cacophonous! (Don't you love the sound of that word? I read it in a book. It means loud and raucous.) They've known each other since they were babies. And they're similar in at least three ways — they're short, they have brown hair, and their lives could be made into miniseries. Sad beginnings, happy endings.

When Mary Anne was an infant, her mom died. Her dad was devastated. He couldn't even think of raising a baby just then. So he sent poor little Mary Anne to live with her grandparents temporarily. Well, guess what? *He* thought it was temporary, but they didn't. They refused to return her. They didn't believe he could handle single parenthood. Well, no *way* was he going to listen to that. He finally convinced them to give Mary Anne back, but the experience scared him. He thought he had to be Mr. Perfect Parent. To him, that meant being super-strict. Right up through the beginning of seventh grade, Mary Anne had to go to bed early, wear her hair in pigtails, keep her phone calls short, and dress in little girl clothes.

When I joined the BSC, Mary Anne looked like Little Bo Peep. Slowly her dad started loosening up a little and letting Mary Anne dress her age. And then her life completely changed. Why? Because Mr. Spier found TRUE LUV. It began when Dawn Schafer joined the BSC. Dawn grew up in California.

But when her parents divorced, Dawn's mom decided to move to Stoneybrook, because she'd grown up here. And guess who was the love of Mrs. Schafer's life in high school? Mary Anne's dad! So Dawn and Mary Anne played matchmaker, and they found that the old flame was still burning. So much crying went on at the Schafer/Spier wedding, I think the church had to change the carpet.

Anyway, Mary Anne and Dawn became stepsisters, and the Spiers moved into the Schafers' farmhouse. (What a cool place. It's two hundred years old, and a secret passageway runs from Dawn's bedroom to a barn.)

Dawn just came back from an extended visit to California. Her dad still lives there, with his new wife and Dawn's ten-year-old brother, Jeff. (Jeff was miserable after moving to Stoneybrook, so Mrs. Schafer let him return to his dad.) Can you imagine an eighth-grade girl convincing her parents — and school — to let her transfer, and then return home? Well, that was what Dawn did. She had a great time, too. She worked with a baby-sitting club out there, and was maid of honor at her dad's wedding.

Dawn is easygoing, intense, open-minded, and opinionated. Sound like a bunch of contradictions? That's Dawn. She's superpassionate about protecting the environment, and she refuses to eat red meat or sugary foods. But she doesn't scream at the sight of Claudia's junk food. And she doesn't lecture. (Well, not to us. She does sometimes go overboard with people she doesn't know so well.)

If you were at a BSC meeting, the first thing you'd notice about Dawn is her hair. It's white-blonde, and down to her waist. (She also has light, freckled skin and dresses in loose, comfortable clothes.) She is our alternate officer, which means she takes over for anyone who's absent.

Now you know about all the regular eighth-grade members of the BSC. Jessi and Mal, as I mentioned before, are in sixth. We call them junior officers, because they're not allowed to baby-sit away from their own homes at night (and boy, do they complain about *that*). In fact, complaining about their parents is one of the main things they have in common. Here are some others: (1) they love to read (especially horse books), (2) they have major talent (Jessi's a ballet dancer and Mal writes and illustrates her own stories), and (3) each is the oldest kid in her family.

Otherwise, they're different. For one thing, Mal's white and Jessi's black. Jessi moved here from a racially mixed town in New Jersey (Mal has lived in Stoneybrook all her life). I'm sorry to say that the Ramsey family faced some really stupid prejudice when they arrived here. Fortunately things have smoothed out since then.

Oh, another major difference between Mal and Jessi is family size. Mallory has *seven* younger brothers and sisters. (When I feel sad about being an only child, I think of her.) Jessi has one younger brother and one younger sister.

Did I mention our associate members? Their names are Logan Bruno and Shannon Kilbourne. Shannon lives in Kristy's neighborhood and goes to a private school, Stoneybrook Day. She's involved in all kinds of extracurricular stuff, but she managed to fill in as alternate officer while Dawn was away.

Logan is a really cute, charming guy with a Southern accent. He's from Louisville, Kentucky (and that's "Loo-uh-vulle," not "Loo-ee-ville," according to Logan). He's also Mary Anne's steady boyfriend, and a terrific sitter. Logan plays after-school sports, which is the main reason he can't attend meetings regularly. Also his friends tease him mercilessly about being a baby-sitter.

Yes, it's true. Oh, well, you know *boys*.

They can't all be wonderful.

Although some can.

Like you know who. As the phone rang again, and another job was assigned, I found myself daydreaming about Robert. About our bike trip. About the concerned look on his face when I fell. The way he held me as he helped me up.

"Uh, Earth to Stacey," Dawn's voice said.

Kristy was making kissing noises.

"Tee hee hee," said Jessi and Mal. I heard one of them whisper "Anastasia Fantasia." (Was that what they were tittering about, Claudia's painting of me? So mature.)

I snapped out of my thoughts. "What?"

"We thought we'd lost you, that's all," Kristy remarked, smirking at Mary Anne. "To dreams of your true lovey-poo."

True lovey-poo?

Puh-leeze.

Mary Anne was all red. Mal and Jessi were now in hysterics.

I kept my cool.

I realized, of course, that some people just don't get it. And you have to wonder if they ever will.

CHAPTER 3

*C*lack.

At first I barely noticed the noise coming from the Johanssens' den.

Clack. Clack.

I was sitting in the kitchen, in Homework Limbo. You know the feeling. You've been working too long, you're bored, and suddenly your eyes start to cross and your body feels numb.

Clack. Clack. Clack.

Okay, now I noticed. I snapped back to reality. I had been at Charlotte's house for two hours. Char had gone upstairs to do *her* homework.

She was in the den now, so she must have finished. Which wasn't too surprising. Charlotte is one of the smartest kids I've ever met. And sweetest, too. I absolutely adore her. We call each other "almost sisters," although you'd never mistake us for the real thing. She has gorgeous, thick, chestnut brown hair. When I first met her, she was this painfully shy, sad-faced seven-year-old. Now she's eight and much more outgoing. (Her mom says I brought her out of her shell, but that's an exaggeration.)

Clack. Clack.

What was she doing in there? I stood up and walked into the den. Charlotte was standing by a bookcase, her arms loaded with videotapes. A small pile of tapes was on the floor beside her.

"Hi," I said.

"Good-bye," she mumbled. "Miss your chips." (At least that's what it sounded like.)

"Huh?"

Charlotte spun around. "Oh, hi, Stacey!"

"Good-bye *what*?" I asked.

She held up a videotape. "Mr. Chips. It's the name of this video. I'm alphabetizing my mom and dad's tapes."

"Oh."

I turned to leave. Obviously that seemed important to her then.

In my mind, I went over the things Dr. Johanssen had asked me to do: Take Charlotte outdoors for awhile (done), fix her a snack (done), see that she does her homework (done), and make sure she practices her piano.

"Charlotte?" I called into the den.

"Have you seen *Lassie Come Home*?" Charlotte replied.

"Uh, yes." I was back in the den now, and Charlotte was holding up the video. "Shouldn't you be —"

"Wasn't that sad when Lassie came walking into the house, all skinny and limping?"

"Ohhhh." I remembered the scene. "I cried when I saw him. And when he went to the school —"

"You *cried*? That was the happy part!" Charlotte quickly put the video on the shelf and held up *The Secret Garden*. "The 'The' doesn't count."

"What?"

"When you alphabetize. See, this goes under *S*. Right after *Safety in Hospital Procedures*."

Uh-huh. Now my baby-sitter antenna was picking up a major Avoidance signal.

"Right, Charlotte. Um, when you're done, will you practice the piano?"

"Sure."

I left her to her project and returned to my science homework.

In the middle of some fascinating news about plant mitochondria, I heard a crash in the bathroom.

I ran down the hall and opened the bathroom door. Charlotte was standing on a stool by the sink, staring at a broken bottle on the floor.

The place smelled as if the walls had been washed with Polo.

"Sorry," Charlotte squeaked.

"What happened?" I asked, stooping to pick up the bigger pieces of glass.

"Well, I was just organizing the cabinet," Charlotte replied. "I mean, everything was so crowded and dusty. Mom always complains about it."

Her brow was creased with concern. I smiled at her and said, "Now you know what to get your dad for his birthday."

As I ran into the kitchen for a sponge, a broom, and a Dustbuster, I heard Charlotte say, "They're going to kill me."

I carefully wiped up the aftershave and the little pieces of glass. "Char, what's with all this organizing?" I asked. "Are you trying to —"

"I'll get you a paper bag!" Charlotte blurted out. She ran out of the bathroom.

Definitely a case of piano-lessonitis. Which surprised me. Char had started taking lessons recently, and she seemed to enjoy them. She'd even played a few pieces for me once. Willingly.

So what had happened?

"Char," I said as she returned with the bag, "have you lost interest in the piano?"

"Nope."

"Will you practice after we clean up? No more organizing?"

"Yup."

I put the pieces of glass into the bag. I was beginning to reek. I was sure my clothes would smell like men's cologne forever. And so would the Johanssens' bathroom.

Afterward I escorted Charlotte to the living room. She slowly walked to the portable electric piano her parents had bought her, which was against the wall near the sofa. With a big sigh, she sat on the stool. It had a round seat you can spin to adjust the height.

Charlotte frowned. "Too high," she said. She climbed off and spun the seat a few times.

She sat again. "Too low."

Off.

Spin, spin, spin.

On.

"Too high again."

This went on for a few minutes until I helped her get it just right.

Then she started playing. I turned back to my homework.

The music stopped.

"I have to go to the bathroom," Charlotte said, racing by me.

She disappeared down the hallway. Polo gusted through the house once more.

Fortunately, no human could remain in that bathroom too long. Charlotte exited and ran back to the piano.

I settled back into my homework, to a song called "Here We Go, Up a Row, to a Birthday Party." Which lasted about one minute.

Plink. Plink. Plink. Plink. Now Char was playing the same note over and over.

In mid-plink she called out, "Does that sound out of tune?"

"Uh, Charlotte —"

Plink. Plink. "Maybe we should call the piano tuner. It could be broken."

Patiently I closed my notebook. I walked into the living room with my nicest baby-sitter smile. "Char, you don't want to practice, do you?"

Charlotte stared at the keyboard, her hands in her lap.

I sat on the floor next to the piano. "Do you really hate playing?"

"No," she said softly.

"Then why don't you just do your lesson?"

"Well, I just . . ." Charlotte was head-to-toe fidgets — head-scratching, leg pumping, eye-darting. This was not like her. "I stink."

"No, you don't, Charlotte. You sound wonderful. Even *Mozart* started out the way you

27

did, with exercises and simple songs."

"How do you know about Mozart?"

Great, McGill. Open mouth, insert foot. "Well, he had to start somewhere."

"Besides, I'm scared," Charlotte said.

"Scared about what?"

Tears were forming in her eyes. "A recital! My teacher's making me play in a recital!"

Aha. So *that* was it.

Charlotte lowered her head. Her hair fell across her face. "She has them twice a year. I asked her if beginners have to play, and she said yes."

"When is it?"

"In about a month." Under her hair, I heard a sniffle. "She is so mean!"

I felt really bad for Charlotte. Even though she's not as shy as she used to be, she hates to perform. "You know, no one expects you to be perfect, Charlotte."

"I don't care! All these people will be staring at me. And I make so many mistakes."

What could I say? If I were in her shoes, I'd probably feel the same way.

So I stood up and put my arm around her. She let her head sink into my shoulder. "I wish you could be there, Stacey," she said.

"I'm not invited?"

Charlotte sat up. "You would come?"

"Well, *sure!*"

"Will you sit in front with my parents so I can see you?"

"Okay."

"Promise?"

"Promise."

"All right." With a big sigh, she looked at her music on the piano. "This is a dumb song."

But she started playing it.

Or trying. As I walked back to the kitchen, I could hear some real clinkers.

Hmmm. Maybe Charlotte was right.

Maybe she wasn't going to be another Mozart, after all.

Oh, well, he had bad hair, anyway.

I went to the bathroom, found two Polo-scented cotton balls to put in my ears, and returned to my homework.

CHAPTER 4

Saturday

I sat for the Pikes last night, and I had a great time. Really. (Don't worry, Stacey. I'm not just saying that. I didn't mind subbing for you at all.)

Well, guess what? It's show biz time again at the Pike house....

Okay, just so you don't get the wrong impression, let me say this: I do not often back out of baby-sitting jobs. I am conscientious. I am hard-working. I am reliable.

I am also, however, human. And *once in awhile*, something comes up.

On Friday evening, it did.

Here's what happened. I was home, just back from the BSC meeting and all prepared to go to the Pikes', when the phone rang.

"Hello?" I said innocently, picking it up.

"Hi." It was Robert. "Don't eat dinner."

I laughed. "Why not?"

"Wayne, Sheila, Alex, and Andi are going to Pizza Express. Want to go?"

Boy, did that sound fun. Sheila MacGregor sits behind me in homeroom, Alex Zacharias and Andi Gentile are two of my newest friends, and you already know about Wayne.

But duty is duty. Sigh.

"Ohhhh, I can't," I said. "I have to baby-sit."

"Okay, that's cool —"

Now, imagine two thought balloons over my head. In one: an evening with seven screaming kids. In the other: me eating pizza with my boyfriend and four of the funniest, coolest kids in my school.

Well, wouldn't *you* be tempted?

Hmmmm. Not long before, I was able to get Mary Anne and Jessi to cover me on two jobs I missed, no problem. It couldn't hurt to try again.

"Wait," I said. "I'll see if I can find someone to sub."

"Yeah?"

"Maybe. I'll call you right back."

I hung up, then called Dawn and Mary Anne's and asked if one of them would take the Pike kids.

Mary Anne practically gasped. "Oh, no! Is it your diabetes, Stacey? Are you okay?"

No diabetes. Just pizza. Boy, did my reason sound stupid all of a sudden. "I'm fine. Something . . . important came up. That's all."

"Oh." Mary Anne sounded skeptical. "Stace, that's the third job you've missed in —"

"Just this one time, Mary Anne," I said.

"All right, hang on. Let me talk to Dawn." I heard the two of them in the background, then Mary Anne came back on the line. "Okay, I can do it, Stacey."

"Thanks! I'll pay you back, Mary Anne!"

I felt a little sneaky. But I hadn't really lied or anything.

And I was glad Mary Anne was the sub. I could return the favor someday if she wanted to go out with Logan.

I called Robert right back. I told him I'd meet him at Pizza Express in an hour.

At the Schafer/Spier house, Mary Anne was quickly getting ready to go to the Pikes'. Dawn wandered into her room and asked, "What happened to Stacey?"

Mary Anne shrugged. "An emergency. She didn't say."

"Emergency?" Dawn repeated.

"Mm-hm."

Dawn was awfully quiet. She didn't seem satisfied with the explanation.

Mary Anne knew what Dawn was thinking. But, nice person that she is, Mary Anne ran downstairs and left for the Pikes'.

She was almost there when she heard a howl.

At first she thought a coyote was loose in the neighborhood. Then another howl joined in. And another. And Mary Anne realized where the sounds were coming from.

The Pike house, 134 Slate Street, had become a wolf den.

"Aw-rooo!" came the first voice.

"Ow! Ow! Owwwwwwww!" answered a second.

"*Stop it!*" screamed the voice of Vanessa Pike.

With a deep sigh, Mary Anne rang the doorbell.

Ever hear seven kids run for a front door at once? No? Well, then, ever been in an earthquake? Same thing.

Adam Pike flung the door open. "Yo, where's Stacey?" was his greeting.

"Mom said she couldn't come," Byron Pike informed him.

"Yeah, Adam, where were you when they handed out brains?" Jordan Pike asked.

"Somewhe-e-e-ere, over the rainbo-o-o-ow . . ." drifted Vanessa's singing voice from upstairs.

"*Aw-rooooo!*" cried Adam, rearing back his head.

"Adaammm," warned Mallory, who was standing behind her siblings.

"Adam, stop it!" Mrs. Pike said sharply, bustling into the room.

"Yeah!" Vanessa echoed from upstairs.

"Hey, it wasn't just *me!*" Adam protested.

Mary Anne recognized a Phase I in the Pike house: Absolute Pandemonium. (Phases II and III are a bit easier: Total Chaos and Constant Mayhem.)

The Pikes, as you can guess, require at least two sitters. Fortunately one sitter is already built in — Mallory.

The next oldest Pikes are Adam, Jordan, and

Byron. They are ten-year-old triplets. (Yikes!) Vanessa was born next (she's nine now), then Nicky (eight), Margo (seven), and Claire (five).

"Hello, Mary Anne," Mrs. Pike said. "Nicky and Margo wanted to make pizza tonight. Mallory will show you where the ingredients are. See you later."

As she shot out the door, Nicky yelled out, "Pizza, dudes!"

Clomp, clomp, clomp, clomp. Vanessa was running down the stairs. "Now?"

"Want to help make it?" Nicky asked.

"Make it? No way! Call me when you're done." *Clomp, clomp, clomp, clomp.*

Margo, Nicky, and Claire raced into the kitchen. Mallory shouted after them, "Wash your hands first!"

The triplets sat on the living room couch, and Adam began shuffling a deck of cards on the coffee table.

"Okay, pick a card, any card," Adam announced to his brothers.

Mary Anne watched Adam do his card trick. Above them, Vanessa's voice rang out: "If happy little bluebirds fly beyond the rainbow . . ."

"What's she doing?" Mary Anne asked Mallory.

Mal rolled her eyes. "Singing along to a tape of *The Wizard of Oz*. She's in love with it."

On the sofa, Adam drew a card from the middle of the deck and thrust it in front of Jordan with a flourish. "Your card," he announced, "was the ace of diamonds."

"Whoa!" Jordan exclaimed. "How did you do that?"

"My turn! My turn!" Byron yelled.

From the kitchen, Margo's voice called, "Nicky dropped the dough!"

Enough magic. Mary Anne and Mallory ran for the kitchen.

The pizza dough, fortunately, was wrapped in plastic and wax paper. It looked like a big, white blob on the floor.

"Ew! Ew!" Claire squealed.

"It's just dough, silly," Nicky explained.

With a grin, Claire started dancing around the kitchen and singing, "Doe, a deer, a female deer . . ."

"Not that kind of dough!" Margo said.

Mary Anne calmly picked up the blob. As she unwrapped it, Mallory placed a wooden cutting board on the kitchen counter.

"Okay, someone has to flatten it first," Mary Anne said. She plopped the dough on the board.

Immediately Margo and Nicky dragged chairs to the counter.

"One at a time," Mallory insisted, pulling a rolling pin out of a drawer.

Margo and Nicky ignored the instructions and the rolling pin. They started slapping the dough with their hands.

Whack-whack-whack-whack!

Claire began a crazy dance, arms flailing.

The triplets ran into the room. As they stared at Claire, her dancing became wilder and wilder.

"What are you doing?" Adam asked.

"Dancing, Adam-silly-billy-goo-goo," Claire replied.

"That's not dancing," Jordan said. "This is." He began heaving his shoulders, bouncing, and chopping the air with his arms.

Mal and Mary Anne could barely keep themselves from cracking up.

Soon Adam grabbed a couple of spoons and began banging them in rhythm. Byron disappeared, then returned, blowing on a harmonica.

"Guys," Mallory warned. *"Guys!"*

The pizza dough looked like a moon landscape. Claire was bumping into chairs, whirling around like an out-of-control windup toy. Mal stood there, feeling more and more frustrated.

And then Vanessa appeared at the kitchen door, totally bewildered.

"Sing!" Claire urged her.

"It's the pizza dance, the pizza dance," Vanessa sang to a made-up tune. "Cheese on your head and ants in your pants. . . ."

Margo shrieked with laughter. Claire fell to the floor, dizzy. Jordan tried to do a split and knocked over a kitchen chair.

Mary Anne was giggling so hard, her eyes were watering. "This isn't baby-sitting," she said. "This is like watching a show."

"Yeah," Jordan piped up. "And it's called Jordan and the Shrimps."

"Adam and the Ants," Adam suggested.

"The Blooshi Gagas!" Claire exclaimed.

"Uh, excuse me?" Mallory said, raising an eyebrow.

Claire collapsed in hysterics at her own humor.

Mary Anne was lost in thought. The Pikes had been involved in a talent show before. Maybe it was time for another.

"You guys," she said. "I think I sense talent show fever again!"

Adam looked as if she'd asked him to bite a sweat sock. But Jordan's eyes lit up. "Yeah! Could Buddy Barrett be in it? You should see his imitation of Sylvester the Cat!"

"And Jake Kuhn could do magic tricks," Margo suggested.

"*I'll* do the magic tricks," Adam retorted.

"And I can be, like, the boss," Byron said.

Vanessa put her hands on her hips. "No

way. I'm the one who knows the most —"

"Whoa," Mallory interrupted. "Let's not talk about bosses."

"You can be in charge of it, Mary Anne," Margo suggested.

Mallory laughed. "I don't think one person could handle you guys."

"We could ask the BSC to help out this time," Mary Anne said.

"*Yeah!*" the Pike kids cried.

Like a herd of small wildebeest, they barreled upstairs to begin planning.

As for the pizza, guess who ended up making it?

I'll give you a hint: no one under the age of eleven.

CHAPTER 5

My mom raced into my bedroom, holding a pair of crisp, turquoise, light-wool slacks. "Here they are!"

"Zzhuh pheshum?" I replied, then took a barrette out of my mouth. "Did you press them?"

"I used the steamer." Mom carefully laid the pants on the bed. "I'll scream if you dribble tomato sauce on them."

"*Mo-om.*"

With a smile, Mom ducked out the door. "Have a great time . . . and you're welcome!"

Oops. "Oh! Thanks for steaming the pants!"

I was a wreck. I wasn't thinking straight. My hair was limp, I had a pimple next to my right nostril, and one of my fingernails had split.

Maybe if I'd had more time, I wouldn't have felt so frantic. But you know boys. To them, it's fine to go out in whatever they've been wearing all day.

At the moment, that didn't seem like a bad idea.

I quickly made myself look like a human being. Then I pulled on my pants and ran downstairs. Mom was doing some work at the kitchen table.

"Can you see my pimple?" I asked.

"Which one?" Mom said with a straight face.

"Mom!"

"Just joking! You look sensational. Pizza Express won't know what hit it. Ready to go?"

"Yup!"

We put on our coats and went out to the car. I kept an eye on the Pikes' backyard, which is visible from ours. Fortunately everyone was inside. No one could see my getaway.

Relax, I told myself. You found a sub. You're not committing a crime.

Some people are born drivers. My mom is not one of them. Being chauffered by her is not for the faint-hearted. Or faint-stomached.

By the time we made it to Pizza Express, she had yelled at a truck driver, almost run a stop sign she was *sure* had never been there before, and been honked at twice for straddling lanes. (I'm used to this by now. It's not her fault, really. In NYC, she hardly ever had to drive.)

Pizza Express was jumping. I could hear the jukebox from the parking lot. As I opened the front door, I saw Robert waving at me from a table near the far wall.

"Hi!" I called out.

The tables and booths were jam-packed. I wound my way across the floor, saying hello to the people I knew. Waiters and waitresses darted past me. The smell of pepperoni, cheese, and tomatoes was making my stomach grumble. (Luckily, the music was drowning it out.)

Robert's huge smile was like a magnet.

"Hey, Stace, what's up?" asked Alex, standing up to let me sit next to Robert on a banquette seat.

"Hope you're hungry," Sheila said. "We ordered."

Before I could say a thing, a waitress arrived with two humongous pizzas — one with extra cheese and pepperoni, the other with pineapple slices.

Yes, pineapple. The idea sounded revolting, sort of like lemon milk, or chocolate asparagus.

"Try it," Andi said. "You'll be surprised."

"Can you?" Robert asked softly, his brow creased. "You know, because of the sugar in the pineapple?"

When you're diabetic, you get used to reminding people about it. Even good friends will offer you candy, completely forgetting. But not Robert. He is so thoughtful. He reminds *me*.

"Pineapple's okay," I said. "In moderation."

"But on *pizza*, she's not so sure," Sheila remarked.

I picked up a slice and took a bite.

"Drumroll, please," Alex said with a dead serious voice.

You know what? It was fabulous. I ate two slices.

We started a craze. The table next to us ordered a pineapple pizza, and then the table next to them.

"If we order one with sushi on top, you think they'll copy us, too?" Sheila asked.

"Squid," I suggested.

"With Alka-Seltzer on the side," Wayne added.

Robert started signaling the waitress.

"Don't you dare!" I said.

We all cracked up. Jokes started flying. Then we drifted into small conversations — about movies, clothes, politics, sports, you name it.

I found out that Alex loves New York, and often stays with an aunt who lives in my old neighborhood. I learned that Andi had had a career as a baby model, and her parents had put away a college fund out of her earnings.

⟨ Everyone was talking about such interesting stuff. I don't know how we managed to finish those pizzas, but we did, and ordered another. And every now and then, Robert would say something incredibly sweet. Or put his arm around me. Or give me a kiss.

You know what? Not one person giggled or made a babyish comment.

It was a magical night. I was sooo grateful to Mary Anne.

I don't know when I began to feel someone was watching me.

Maybe when I thought I spotted someone ducking behind a booth. Maybe when I saw someone who was wearing a hood run into the bathroom.

I didn't register those things very strongly. Until the jukebox stopped.

I figured I'd play some tunes. I stood up and asked my friends for requests. Then I glanced toward the box and saw somebody duck behind it. Somebody wearing a hooded down coat.

Hmm. I turned back to the table. I carefully wrote down the songs everyone wanted to hear. I could tell Robert sensed something was wrong.

Then I spun around.

A pair of blue eyes and a flash of blonde hair disappeared behind the jukebox.

"I think I'm being watched," I whispered.

"*What?*" Robert said.

I marched across the room to the jukebox. Crouching down on the far side of it was Dawn Schafer.

"Dawn?" I said. "What are you doing?"

"Hi, Stacey," Dawn replied, standing up. Her face turned bright red as she looked me in the eye. "So, you had an emergency tonight, huh?"

"You *are* spying on me!"

"I thought you'd be with Robert," Dawn said calmly. "At least you could have admitted it, instead of lying to Mary Anne."

"I did not lie!"

"I know you have a boyfriend, but Mary Anne does, too, you know. At least she honors her responsibility to the Baby-sitters Club!"

Dawn had definitely said that too loudly.

"Yeah, you bad girl!"

Oh, lord. Alan Gray's voice. Mr. Immature of the Eighth Grade. He would have to be there.

The whole place was staring at us now. Giggles were breaking out all around. Robert and my friends looked shocked. Sheila was trying to stifle a laugh.

I wanted to melt. Evaporate. Change my

identity and move to Antarctica.

"Excuse me," Dawn said. Her chin held high, she walked past me and out the front door. With her hood, her six-foot knit scarf, her down coat and L. L. Bean boots, she looked like Nanook of the North.

I slunk back toward my table. All I could think about was the last time a friend had seriously spied on me. I was living in New York, and my friend was hiding behind a bush in Central Park. We were seven years old.

Which was about how old I felt right then.

Robert had this sympathetic look in his eye when I sat down. "What was that all about?"

"The Baby-sitters Club international spy ring," Sheila remarked.

"I thought Mary Anne covered your sitting job," Robert said.

"She did," I replied. "I just didn't tell her exactly why I couldn't go."

Wayne let out a low whistle. "I guess they take themselves seriously, huh?"

"A little . . . *too* seriously, maybe?" Sheila commented. "I mean, get a life!"

What could I say? I couldn't disagree. But I couldn't agree, either. The BSC members had been my friends, my *best* friends, since I had first moved to Stoneybrook.

Do best friends embarrass you like that? Do

they act like babies? Make you feel like a traitor for having a boyfriend?

I thought about my former best friend in New York, Laine Cummings. When I moved to Stoneybrook, she became so snobby. I realized I had grown out of my friendship with her. It was painful to admit it at the time, but I hardly think of her anymore.

And then an awful question popped into my head. Something I hadn't thought of before.

Was I growing out of the Baby-sitters Club?

CHAPTER 6

"No, a little to the right," my mom said.

Robert and I pushed. Mom's new exercise machine scraped against the linoleum floor as we moved it closer to the basement wall.

Grunt, grunt, puff, puff. I don't know about you, but I hate manual labor.

I must admit, though, I hate it a little less when Robert's around.

"How's that, Mrs. McGill?" Robert asked.

"Fine," Mom said with a sigh. "Now I just have to learn to use it."

"No problem," Robert replied. "I'll show you."

As he sat on the machine's padded seat, I casually looked at my watch.

Five-twenty-eight.

Yikes!

It was Monday, and I had two minutes to make it to the BSC meeting — which is at least a six-minute trip from my house.

"Oops, I have to go to Claud's!" I announced, dashing upstairs.

"I'll go with you!" Robert said, following me. " 'Bye, Mrs. McGill!"

"Sorry!" Mom called out. "I didn't mean to —"

I didn't hear the rest. Robert and I were flying.

I had vowed to be at this meeting on time. After what happened on Friday, I knew I'd be in trouble. Dawn had had a whole weekend to tell everybody the news.

I needed wings. Better yet, a time warp.

My bad deeds were piling up. A few latenesses, a few skipped jobs . . . I could already hear Kristy's lecture.

Lecture? Iron shackles, maybe.

Robert and I raced down Elm Street and up Bradford Court. We said a quick good-bye in front of the Kishis' house. I barged inside, ran upstairs, and hurried through Claudia's bedroom door.

Facing me were the Six Sisters of Doom: Grim, Grumpy, Glum, Sullen, Somber, and Bleak.

"Hi," I said with my friendliest smile.

Shift, hrrmph, grumble, cough, was the response.

"Sorry I'm late," I continued. "See, my mom was installing this exercise machine —"

Kristy cleared her throat. "It isn't just *this* lateness, Stacey."

"Oh?" I must have been nervous. My voice sounded like Tweetie Bird's.

"You've been on another planet lately," Kristy continued. "I mean, do you want to be in the club?"

"Of course I do!" I replied.

"Well, you don't act like it. It's bad enough you're breaking rules about subbing —"

"Kristy, I'm sorry —"

"But you tricked Mary Anne," Kristy barged on. "I think you owe her an apology."

Mary Anne was looking at the bedspread. Her hair was falling in front of her face. "No, it's all right," she said.

I could tell it wasn't.

I had been so mad at Dawn over the weekend, I never considered Mary Anne's point of view. At least I could have been honest with her. Her feelings do get hurt easily.

"I'm sorry, Mary Anne," I said. "I should have told you the truth."

"Really, it's okay," Mary Anne repeated.

But Kristy had that *I'm just getting started* look in her eyes. "You know, if all of us skipped jobs every time a boyfriend called, what kind of club would this be?"

"Kristy," Claudia said, "she apologized.

50

Ease up. Stacey's not the only one who was sneaky."

Dawn sat bolt upright. "Hey, I was just curious. I didn't mean to —"

"I know, I know," Claud cut in. "I'm not trying to blame you, either. It's just that we're supposed to be friends, right? We all make mistakes. Let's forgive, forget, and have some Goobers."

She jumped off her bed, pulled some books off her bookcase, and took out a huge bag filled with boxes of candy.

"Yum!" Jessi exclaimed, reaching for a box.

Next Claudia pulled a bag of pretzels from behind her bed. "For Dawn and Stacey."

"Whole wheat?" Dawn asked.

"I don't know," Claudia answered, "but they look disgusting, so they must be good for you."

Everyone grabbed for a snack, and *poof*. That was it. End of argument.

Leave it to Claud.

But as we munched away, I felt pretty awful. Mary Anne is the last person in the world I would ever take advantage of.

I vowed to be more conscientious. Still, I couldn't help thinking: the BSC should be a little more lenient. I hadn't exactly been a model member, but I had found substitute sitters when I needed to. And being late to meetings is bad, but it's not a capital crime. I mean, this was the Baby-sitters Club, not the Knights of the Round Table.

Then I thought about the kids at Pizza Express on Friday. They would never be as rigid as Kristy. None of them would spy from behind a jukebox, the way Dawn had done. None of them would treat a casual date as if it were high treason. I mean, we were all pretty much the same age, but my new friends seemed older than the BSC members.

Kristy was tossing Goobers in the air and catching them in her mouth. Claudia was looking for something under her mattress. Dawn was examining a pretzel intently. Mary Anne was shooting me sad puppy-dog looks. Jessi and Mal were playing Hangman on the floor.

I felt out of place.

Don't be a snob, Stacey, I told myself. Friends are friends.

"Oooh!" Mary Anne burst out. "I almost forgot. Uh, I move to open discussion on a kids' talent show."

"Okay," Kristy replied. "I mean, motion granted."

Move to open discussion? Motion granted? Puh-leeze. (Honestly, I don't know why Kristy requires all this super-seriousness.)

Mary Anne and Mallory described the sitting job at the Pikes' — the pizza making, dancing, and singing.

"They're such hams," Mallory continued. "They want to involve all the neighborhood kids," Mallory continued. "You know, like a spring project. Kids could do imitations, comedy acts, songs, magic, whatever."

"It's a big job, so the BSC would have to help out," Mary Anne added.

"I think it's a fantastic idea," Dawn said.

Kristy raised her eyebrows as if to say, Well, maybe not fantastic. "What's your plan? Have you thought about scheduling, or supplies, or advertising, or admission price?"

Mallory shrugged. "Not yet."

"No admission," Mary Anne said. "It'll just be for friends and family."

"Oh, Becca will love this!" Jessi squealed.

"Wait, let's have a show of hands," Kristy announced. "All in favor of club involvement?"

Everyone raised a hand. Jessi raised two.

Kristy announced, "It's unanimous. Motion carried."

As if we didn't know.

"Yea!" Jessi leaped up. "I'll choreograph!"

"Should we, like, limit this or invite all the kids?" Dawn asked.

"Ugh," Claudia moaned. "This could really get out of hand."

Kristy shrugged. "No problem. Just have auditions. A lot of the kids won't show up. Whoever does can be in the show."

(She may be bossy, but she does have good ideas.)

"Maybe Charlotte will play the piano," I suggested.

"Uh, let's stick to the *w*'s, okay?" Kristy said.

"The what?" I asked.

"We did the *what* already," Kristy replied, as if she were speaking to a two-year-old. "Now we need the *when* and *where*."

"Oh," I said. (Duh.)

"Maybe we could use our barn," Mary Anne said.

Rrrrring!

A phone call interrupted our plans. Then two or three more followed. We didn't have a chance to do much more talent show planning.

No one brought up the Robert fiasco again, either. That was a big relief.

But I still felt bad about what I'd done to Mary Anne. I wanted to make it up to her soon.

After the meeting, Dawn stayed to gab with Claudia, so Mary Anne left alone.

"I'll walk you partway," I said to her.

"Great," Mary Anne replied with a smile. "And don't apologize."

"Huh?"

"I can tell you're worried. But you didn't do such a bad thing."

"Thanks," I replied. "I kind of got carried away."

"Well, we're still bestest of friends."

Bestest of friends?

"Uh-huh," I said.

Mary Anne giggled. "That's what Logan's sister says. Bestest. Isn't it cute?"

"Uh-huh. Um, you want to do something together tomorrow? I was going to go shopping after school."

"Okay! That'll be neat!"

We talked a bit more, then turned our separate ways on Elm Street. As Mary Anne walked off, I noticed a new sticker on her backpack.

A smily kitten with huge eyes, surrounded by fuzzy hearts and the words I ♥ MY KITTY.

I almost gagged.

I mean, really.

I sure hoped she wouldn't take that to the mall the next day.

Oh, well, I could always wear a mask.

CHAPTER 7

Bra
Corduroy pants (on sale)
Ankle socks
Breton red cotton baseball cap
Radishes

That last item on my shopping list was Mom's. She had snuck it in while I was eating breakfast Tuesday morning.

Since Mary Anne and I were going to the outdoor mall after school, Mom figured we could stop at the supermarket.

Moms have a way of doing that.

" 'Bye!" I called out to her as I left for school.

"Don't forget the radishes!" was her farewell.

Sigh. What if I were run over by a truck on the way to school? Mom would always have to live with the fact that her last words to her daughter were "Don't forget the radishes."

As I approached Burnt Hill Road, I saw Mary Anne. She was standing on the corner of Elm Street, waiting for me.

"Hi!" I called out.

"Hi." As we began walking together, Mary Anne said, "Um, Stacey? About our shopping trip this afternoon?"

"I hope you don't mind radishes."

"Huh?"

"Nothing."

She frowned. "Did you remember you're supposed to sit for Charlotte this afternoon?"

Gulp.

"Uh-oh."

"I mean, if Dr. Johanssen called you to cancel or something, that's fine. See, I called Claud to check the record book about something, and she happened to mention —"

"No, you're right," I said. "I am supposed to sit for her. I — I forgot. Ohhhhh, I am so stupid!"

Boy, was Mary Anne furious. She socked me in the jaw, pulled my hair, and refused to talk to me for a month.

You don't believe me, do you?

Good.

You know Mary Anne. She just smiled and said, "That's okay, Stacey. I really didn't need anything, anyway."

Now I really felt like a bonehead. So much for trying to make things up to Mary Anne. First I had been devious with her, and now I was standing her up.

"I'm sorry, Mary Anne," I said. "I'll make it up to you. What about, like, I don't know, Thursday?"

"I have a job."

"Saturday, then? I mean, anytime is fine."

"Don't worry. Really. We'll look in the record book together. We'll figure out a day."

I exhaled. I wanted to be a clam, so I could fold into my shell.

We talked about math the rest of the way to school.

* * *

58

I ended up standing next to Andi in the lunch line that day. "Mmm, cheese balls," she mumbled.

I looked at the little clumps of yellow cheese, covered with chopped nuts. "Yummy," I muttered back.

I followed Andi through the line (avoiding the cheese balls). Together we went to a table near the window. Wayne, Sheila, and Alex were there.

I waved to Kristy and Dawn, who were sitting at the BSC table.

Meaning the table where us BSC members *usually* sit. We're not required to sit there. Sometimes Mary Anne sits with Logan and his friends. No big deal. It's a free country.

Kristy and Dawn stared at me silently, chewing intently on their food. They did not look happy.

I felt self-conscious. I wanted to tell them to lighten up. But maybe I wasn't what was making them look so sour.

It could have been the cheese balls.

Well, I had a great time at lunch. Especially after Robert joined us. (He, by the way, loved the cheese balls. He ate three of them.)

I was stunned when the bell rang. The period felt about five minutes long. We had talked and laughed nonstop.

It was chemistry, I guess. I knew Robert and

I had the same chemistry. Now I was discovering six people could share it, too.

On my way to class, I met up with Mary Anne in the hall.

"So," I said, "did you think about a day for that shopping trip?"

Mary Anne smiled patiently. "The record book's at Claudia's, Stacey. We'll check tomorrow."

"Oh. Right. You're not mad at me, are you? I'm really sorry."

"No. It's okay. Well, I have to go to class."

"Okay. 'Bye."

" 'Bye."

"Don't forget, the winter clearance sales are on now."

"Great!"

With that, we headed to our classes.

I don't know why I was so apologetic. Maybe because I hadn't sat at the BSC table.

I don't know why that seemed like such a big deal.

Sweet sweet sweet sweet sweet SOUR.
Sweet sweet SOUR sweet OUCH sweet sweet.

That is the only way I can think of to describe the piano playing of Charlotte Johanssen. She was practicing as I arrived at her house.

Yes, practicing. Either she'd run out of things to alphabetize or she was adjusting to the idea of the recital.

I hoped the second choice was true.

"Do I sound okay?" she asked.

"Wonderful," I lied. "Keep going."

She did. And boy, did she concentrate. I don't even think she noticed when her mom left.

I was proud of Char. She was really trying. "Yeeaa! Great job!" I cheered.

She looked up blankly. "That's not the end."

Oops.

"Sorry."

I listened patiently to the same notes again and again.

And again.

Soon I began to make out an actual tune.

I have to admit, though. I enjoyed being there. I mean, despite all my problems with the BSC, I like sitting. As Char continued, I tried to figure out a way to prove I was still dedicated. And then I had a brilliant idea.

"Charlotte," I said. "How would you like to be in a talent show?"

Charlotte has extremely pale skin. But when I said those words, she turned a shade of pale I'd never before witnessed.

"Talent show?" she whispered.

"Just a fun thing, with the kids in the neighborhood, and the BSC."

Charlotte was already shaking her head. Her eyes had *Don't even think of it* in them.

"Char," I said, "you're still a little nervous about your recital, right?"

"Yeah."

"Well, look at it this way. The talent show will be informal, just for friends and family and the BSC. It'll be like a practice for the recital. In a friendly environment, where everybody's on your side."

Char was still shaking her head. "I don't know."

"Look, Adam Pike'll be doing silly tricks. Buddy Barrett will probably try to do a comedy act. I bet Vanessa will sing. None of them is a pro. It'll be fun."

Now Charlotte was thinking about it. "Will you be in the audience?"

"Of course!"

"Well . . . maybe."

"Great. Now, which piece do you think you'd play?"

Charlotte leafed through her book. She broke into a smile. "I learned this at my lesson."

She played something that sounded exactly like whatever she had been playing before.

Then she looked up, beaming. "Isn't that one nice?"

"Beautiful!" I replied.

"Then I'll play a major and a minor scale. Listen."

Mission accomplished. Charlotte was going to be in the talent show. I was sure it would help her confidence at the recital.

And help get me out of the BSC doghouse.

Frankly, I was quite proud of myself.

CHAPTER 8

Thursday

Remember my idea about holding auditions for the talent show? I was so sure only a small group of kids would show up. I was positive the shy ones would just ignore us.

I was wrong. Totally, one hundred percent wrong....

Come on, Sari."

"Go ahead, Sari."

"Come back here, Sari."

A dog-training session? No, it was Hannie and Linny Papadakis trying to get their two-year-old sister, Sari, to sing.

They had just arrived at Kristy's house. And they were determined to make Sari a star.

It was Thursday afternoon. Kristy was taking care of David Michael and Emily Michelle. Her stepsiblings, Andrew and Karen, were at their mother's house.

Piece of cake, Kristy thought.

That was before the doorbell rang and the Brewer mansion became Hollywood East.

If you ask me, Kristy should have expected it. By now the entire town of Stoneybrook seemed to know about the talent show. On Wednesday, four parents called during the BSC meeting to find out details. One of them, Mrs. Wilder, actually asked us, "Are all the slots booked?"

The trouble was, we'd been so busy that week, we hadn't really cemented plans for the show, let alone started "booking slots."

Anyway, when Kristy answered the door and saw Hannie and Linny, she figured they wanted to play with David Michael. "David Michael!" she called into the house.

"No!" Linny cried. "Come on, Sari . . . 'Twinkle, twinkle . . .' "

"Emmy," Sari said. "Emmy home?"

"Sari, sing!" Linny commanded.

"No!" Sari shot back.

"She knows all the words," Hannie insisted.

"I'm sure she does," Kristy said with a smile. "But I think maybe she wants to play with Emily."

"Hi!" called David Michael and Emily Michelle, running into the living room.

"Emmy! Emmy!" Sari cried out, jumping up and down.

"Oh, no!" Linny complained. "You spoiled it."

David Michael looked crushed. "Spoiled what?"

Hannie was holding her little sister by the shoulders. " 'Twinkle, twinkle,' " she urged.

Emily Michelle's eyes lit up. " 'Litto 'tar, howa water waddoo are.' "

"No! No! No!" Sari screamed. "Fire trucks!"

Hannie let go. Sari and Emily went toddling away toward the den.

"I know," Linny said. "They can sing it together. A doot!"

"A what?" Kristy asked.

Linny rolled his eyes. "It's when two people sing, Kristy. A doot. D-U-E-T."

"Uh-huh," Kristy replied. "I think it's pronounced *duet*. And we'll be having auditions —"

"Wasn't *that* an audition?" Hannie asked.

She looked so hurt, Kristy didn't have the heart to say no. "Well, I guess so."

"All riiiight!" Linny said. "Now follow me!"

He ran into the den, with Kristy, Hannie, and David Michael close behind. Then Linny pulled a cassette tape out of his pocket and put in into the Brewers' player.

"Watch!"

The song "To Life!" from the musical *Fiddler on the Roof* began blaring. Linny crouched down, crossed his arms, and began kicking his legs. Every few seconds he'd call out, "Hey!" He looked a little like a soccer player with a stomachache.

Sari and Emily, who were playing on the floor with fire engines, stopped and stared.

Then, finally, as the song ended, Linny jumped in the air and fell on his behind. "Yeeoow!"

Sari, Emily, Hannie, and David Michael all burst out laughing.

"That part's hard," Linny said. "But the rest is pretty good, huh? It's the bottle dance. You know, in the video, where all the men dance with bottles on their heads?"

"Mm-hm," Kristy replied. "But where's your bottle?"

Linny looked crestfallen. "I thought this was just an audition."

Kristy laughed. "Okay. You're in, Linny."

"*Yes!*"

Then Kristy had to sit through Hannie's rendition of "Sunrise, Sunset" — all sung on one note.

By this time, David Michael was determined to audition, too. He ran upstairs and got a Daffy Duck puppet. Then he dragged in a stool from the kitchen and put on a "ventriloquist act."

Linny cracked up. "You stink, David Michael! Right, Kristy? He can't be in the show. You can see his lips moving."

"I can so be in the show!" David shot back. "*You* didn't even use a bottle!"

"Whoa, easy guys," said Kristy the Peacemaker. "You can all be in it."

"Yeeeeaah!" the kids shouted. Sari and Emily began jumping up and down, even though they had no idea why.

Ding-dong!

Kristy ran to the door. Maria Kilbourne, Shannon's eight-year-old sister, was standing there, dressed in a tuxedo and top hat. In her right hand was a pair of tap shoes.

"Maria?" Kristy greeted her. "Since when do you tap dance?"

"I just started last month," Maria answered.

"Do you have a cassette player and a hard floor?"

"The den is carpeted," Kristy replied. "How about the basement? It has a tiled floor."

"Okay."

"Okay, kids, downstairs!" Kristy ordered.

As everyone scampered into the basement, Kristy ran to her brother Charlie's room and borrowed his boom box.

She brought it to the basement and put Maria's tape in it.

Linny, Hannie, David Michael, Sari, and Emily Michelle were sitting on the floor, staring at Maria. She had put on her tap shoes and was clacking around noisily.

"And now," Maria announced in a singsong voice, "I shall present a tap combination to 'Puttin' on the Ritz.' "

Linny burst out laughing. "Pudding on a Ritz? That's disgusting!"

"Not a Ritz cracker, dingbat!" Maria said. "It's just a *song*."

"A Ritz is a song," Linny repeated, as if it was the dumbest thing he ever heard.

Maria flicked on the tape. As the song began, she bent her knees and started her routine.

Clackety - clack - stomp - scrape - whap - clackety - smack!

How did she do? Well, according to Kristy,

Maria's steps had nothing to do with the rhythm of the song. She looked like someone trying to stomp on an army of cockroaches.

Kristy adores Maria, but she couldn't wait for the routine to end.

When it did, the kids burst out cheering.

"That was great!" David Michael said. "I want to learn how to do that."

"Looks easy," Linny remarked.

Maria glared at him. "I'd like to see you try it."

"Let me have your shoes, then."

"No way, not with your moose feet!"

Hannie and David Michael roared at that, which made Sari and Emily Michelle giggle.

"Can I be in the show, please please please?" Maria pleaded.

"You bet," Kristy replied.

"Yeaaaaaaa!"

Maria ran upstairs, forgetting to take off her tap shoes. Kristy could hear her clacking all the way out the door and onto the front steps.

And that was only the beginning. A little later, Bill and Melody Korman came over and sang their own duet, "A Whole New World," from *Aladdin*.

Kristy reported that Melody did not live up to her name.

By the time Kristy's mother came home, half

of Stoneybrook had auditioned, and Sari and Emily Michelle were screaming "Twinkle Twinkle Little Star" at the top of their lungs.

By now, everybody wanted to get into the act.

"A Fiesta Burger?" Robert squinted at the Burger Town menu. "What's that?"

"After you eat it, you fall asleep," Andi remarked.

Alex laughed. "That's *siesta*, not *fiesta*."

Andi slapped her forehead. "Oh, no. There goes my perfect score on today's Spanish quiz."

"Very funny," Alex said.

"It has guacamole, salsa, melted cheese, chili, and chips on the side," Wayne said.

"What does?" Robert asked.

"The Fiesta Burger!" Wayne said.

"How do you know?" Sheila asked.

"I just saw one go by."

It was Friday night. Robert, Wayne, Sheila, Alex, Andi, and I were squeezed into a booth meant for four people. We'd decided to go to Burger Town because of their new advertising campaign: DOUBLE-SIZED BURGERS ON FRIDAYS!

Double-sized? That was a nice way of putting it. They were beef mountains.

We all followed Wayne's glance to a plate on a nearby table. I must say, the Fiesta Burger was not a mountain. It was more like a volcano. The guacamole and chili ran down the sides like lava.

It looked horrifying.

"Wow, that's what I'm having!" Robert said. "With steak fries, and some pecan pie à la mode for dessert."

Yes, he was serious.

Sheila smiled. "I'm going to have the Regrub."

"What's that?" I asked.

"Something new," Sheila replied. "It's 'Burger' backward. They fold all the toppings *into* the burger, instead of putting them on the outside."

Ugh. "Um, anybody want to split a regular cheeseburger?" I asked.

"Don't worry," Robert said. "I'll eat whatever you don't finish."

"*Plus* the fiesta monster?"

Robert shrugged. "I'm hungry."

No, he is not fat. Not even close.

Go figure.

Burger Town, as you might guess, is the Fat and Sugar Capital of Stoneybrook. You gain a pound just breathing the air.

So what does Stacey the Diabetic do? The same thing I do at Pizza Express. Stay away from desserts, eat moderately, and watch in awe as Robert Brewster consumes his weight in food while carrying on a conversation.

Robert is amazing. He would eat a dictionary if you covered it with some sauce and put it in a toasted bun.

Anyway, this was the third or fourth time our group of six had gone out together. We'd begun to feel so close and open. That evening, for example, Alex told us his parents had just decided to break up. He was really upset, so we listened and offered whatever help we could.

We were huddled over the table when I spotted Kristy, Mary Anne, and Dawn walking toward us.

"Hey, what's the big secret?" Kristy called out, with a huge grin.

"Oh, hi, guys," I said.

Kristy was wearing mismatched socks, and a sweat shirt with the word KRUSHERS handwritten on the front in thick marker. She made a big show of looking at her watch. "Um, aren't you baby-sitting for the Prezziosos tonight?"

I panicked. The Prezziosos? When did we set that up? I didn't remember it at all.

"Kris*tyyyy*," Mary Anne said.

"Just kidding." Kristy laughed. "Well, see you later."

" 'Bye," Dawn and Mary Anne said.

" 'Bye," my other friends replied.

My heart climbed its way back down from my throat to my chest.

"Are you all right, Stacey?" Andi asked.

"Fine," I said. "Uh, where were we?"

Alex was buttering a roll. "Never mind," he said.

Thank you, Kristy. What a way to kill a conversation.

My three BSC friends were now slipping into a nearby booth. For the first time, I noticed the Mickey Mouse on the back of Mary Anne's shirt, which was grinning stupidly at us.

I wished she hadn't worn that.

I could hear Dawn asking Mary Anne, "Do they have double salads, too, or just cooked cow carcasses?"

"Ewww, Dawn," Mary Anne replied.

Ignore them, half of me was saying.

You snob, said the other half. I was being embarrassed by my best friends, and that wasn't right. Besides, no one at my table seemed to be bothered.

"Ready to order?" asked a waitress, setting down a basket of bread.

"Fiesta Burger," Robert said. "With extra fries."

"Grecian Burger," Alex piped up.

"Bacon Cheeseburger," Andi ordered.

And so on. (I guess Dawn's carcass comment hadn't grossed anyone out.)

As the waitress left, everyone tore into the bread basket. Robert and I grabbed hold of the same long roll. We lifted it out together. Robert said, "Tug-of-war!" and we both pulled.

I ended up with the bigger piece.

"Good work, Stacey," Andi said.

"Tee hee hee hee," Mary Anne Spier's voice tittered.

I looked over to see my three BSC friends staring at our table. Kristy raised her eyebrows and rubbed her index fingers together in a "shame on you" gesture.

Oh, please.

I smiled and tried to ignore them.

But it was tough. A few minutes later I heard another burst of giggles. I looked over to see Kristy sticking straws up her nose.

This time Wayne saw it too. "Really clears your sinuses," he remarked with a smile.

He was being kind.

Our meals arrived quickly. It took a waiter

and a waitress to serve us. (Honestly, at the end of a double burger day, they must look like Arnold Schwarzenegger.)

Robert rolled up his sleeves, gaping at the greenish-brown mound of guacamole, chili, and beef. "How am I supposed to eat this thing?"

"Do they give you a shovel?" Alex asked.

Everyone dug in. Wayne, Andi, and Sheila actually picked theirs up by hand. Robert tried that, but his burger had become . . . well, a *fiesta* all over his plate. He ended up using a fork and knife.

All our talking had made us hungry. No one said a word for about ten minutes. We just stuffed and stuffed.

The place was starting to fill up now. Out of the corner of my eye, I saw Carlos Mendez walk in. He's this movie-star-handsome guy who goes to Stoneybrook High School. He used to go out with Sabrina Bouvier, who goes to SMS.

Well, you should have heard Dawn giggle when he passed by her table. Maybe you did. It was so loud and high-pitched, I'm surprised it didn't shatter glass.

That made Kristy burst out laughing. Unfortunately, she had just taken a drink of soda. Some of it came flying out of her nose.

Which made Dawn and Mary Anne giggle.

"Must have been a good joke," was Wayne's comment.

"It wasn't a joke," Andi explained. "It was a cute guy."

Alex frowned. "They're in *eighth* grade?"

It was an innocent question. He did not mean it sarcastically. But I felt my stomach clench.

"Uh-huh," I said. "I guess they're just in a silly mood tonight."

"Tonight?" Sheila muttered.

Now, *that* was sarcastic.

To tell you the truth, I couldn't blame her.

A waiter had stopped by Kristy's table. I could hear Dawn asking, "Is the vegetarian special grilled in vegetable oil, butter, or lard?"

The waiter pointed to the menu. "Pure canola oil, just as it says there."

"And what about MSG?" Dawn pressed.

Next thing I knew, the waiter was scurrying off to the kitchen and Kristy, with a mischievous look, was shoving a pat of butter in her mouth.

"Ew! Stop, Kristy, that's disgusting!" Dawn cried. "Gross! Gross!"

Why were they doing this to me? Had they always acted like this? Had I just been too stupid to notice it before?

Now Robert was staring at them.

I don't remember much about the rest of the meal. I worked hard to stop looking at Kristy's table, and they did calm down when the food came. Well, except for the fact that Dawn built a little fortress around her plate, using the menus as walls (I guess to keep the meat vibes from reaching her plate).

When we finally left, I gave them a brief good-bye. Very brief.

Robert and I put our arms around each other as we all strolled away from the restaurant.

"I am *stuffed*," Wayne said.

"Me, too," Andi agreed. "How about you, Robo-Stomach?"

Robert turned red and shrugged.

"Aughh! He's ready for another meal!" Wayne cried out.

We joked around for awhile, wandering slowly away from Burger Town. The night was clear and gorgeous, and the chill was beginning to ease up. I took a deep breath. "I can smell spring."

"That's just the exhaust from Burger Town," Andi remarked.

"No, I smell it, too," Robert said. "It's about time. We should celebrate."

"Don't tell me you want to go out for dessert," Sheila said.

"No. I mean, like, a party," Robert replied. "We can have it at my house. Invite everyone."

"Sounds great," Wayne said.

We all agreed.

Then Sheila asked, "Uh, Stacey? No offense, but would you invite . . ." She gestured back toward Burger Town. "You know . . ."

"The members of the Baby-sitters Club?" I asked.

Sheila smiled self-consciously. "I mean, don't take this wrong, but you know, they do act a little . . ."

"Immature," I finished.

"Well, yeah."

"Don't worry," I said. "They don't have to know about it."

You know what? I did not feel guilty saying that. Frankly, I didn't want my BSC friends at the party. It wasn't that I thought they'd embarrass me, exactly. It just wouldn't be a good mix, that's all.

Well, except for Claudia. I mean, she would fit in fine.

The only problem was, I didn't know how I was going to handle that. Could I invite Claudia and not the others?

I didn't need to think about that then. Why spoil the night?

It could wait.

CHAPTER 10

"I'm not hungry," Jamie Newton said. He slumped off his chair and began walking away from the Newtons' kitchen table.

"Gah!" Lucy Newton agreed, dropping her right hand in a plastic bowl full of rice cereal.

"But your mom said you've hardly eaten all day," I told Jamie.

"I wasn't hungry then, either," Jamie replied.

"Well, the sooner you eat, the sooner I can read to you."

Jamie slowly turned back to the table. "All right," he mumbled.

With a grimace, he began eating his plate of semi-warm macaroni and cheese.

Jamie's four and Lucy's not quite a year old. I was sitting for them on Tuesday, four days after Burger Town — and three days before Robert and Stacey's End-of-Winter Party!

That's right. Friday was the big day. How's

that for quick action? You should have heard our planning session at Robert's house on Saturday. It went something like this:

Me: "When should we have the party?"

Robert: "Friday? Here?"

Me: "Your parents won't mind?"

He: "Nah."

Me: "Okay. Let's start calling."

End of planning.

I'm glad Kristy wasn't there. She would have fainted.

We called all our mutual friends, and just about all of them said yes. The last call I made was to Claudia.

I had thought about it a lot. I almost didn't invite her, to be fair to the others in the BSC. But then I thought: What about Claudia? Would it be fair to *her*? I mean, she *is* my best friend. And she fits in great with my other friends. Why should I penalize her by lumping her in with the rest of the BSC?

Claud said yes right away, until I told her I wasn't inviting the other members.

"Why?" she asked. "Doesn't Robert like them?"

"Sure he does," I answered. "It's just that, well, it wouldn't be a good mix, you know? I mean, Jessi and Mal probably wouldn't be allowed to, anyway. And you should have seen the way Kristy and Mary Anne and Dawn acted in Burger Town. I love them and all, but you have to admit they can be socially. . . ."

"Awkward," Claudia said.

"Right."

"Well, Robert's house isn't too near anyone else's, so that helps. I guess we can just keep a low profile about it."

"Absolutely."

Claudia sighed. "Okay, I'll be there."

I was in a fabulous mood all weekend. It was great preparation for my Tuesday baby-sitting job with Jamie the Fusspot.

Slowly Jamie lifted a forkful of macaroni and cheese into his mouth. He chewed it as if it were dried codfish. "Way to go, Jamie!" I said with a smile.

"Gah!" squealed Lucy.

I spooned some more rice cereal into her mouth. She, luckily, had a good appetite.

After a few more minutes of this, Jamie had finished about half his meal. The other half had coagulated into a big orange lump on his plate. I didn't push him. The stuff *was* kind of gross.

For the next hour or so, Jamie pushed around some action figures in the den while I bathed Lucy and put her to bed.

She was asleep halfway through the second verse of "Hush, Little Baby."

I turned on the baby monitor. Then I tiptoed

out of the room and went downstairs into the den. The monitor's receiver was there, so I turned that on, too.

"Okay, Jamie," I said, "get into your pj's and I'll read to you."

As Jamie shuffled toward the stairs, the phone rang.

I picked up the receiver. "Hello, Newton residence."

"Stacey? It's Robert."

"Hi!" I said, settling into a kitchen chair.

"I'm bored," he said. "My parents are out tonight. I finished my homework. Our TV is broken."

"So I was your last resort?" I asked.

"No! I didn't mean that!"

I couldn't help giggling. "Oh, all right. I'll keep you company."

Technically, BSC members are not supposed to have long phone conversations while working. It distracts the sitter from the kids, and it ties up the phone (which should be free in case the parents need to call).

I could hear Jamie opening his chest of drawers. Through the monitor I could also hear baby snores from Lucy's room. Everything was under control. And I was pretty sure the Newtons had Call Waiting.

A *short* conversation couldn't hurt.

We talked about our shopping trip for the party — when we would do it (Thursday), what we would buy (chips, pretzels, soda, juice, the usual stuff) — and the kinds of music we'd play (he likes metal and alternative, but I think house music works better at a party).

Then Robert told me a few horrible jokes he'd heard from Wayne.

I told him some much funnier ones I'd heard from Claudia.

I kept an ear open to the baby monitor, but everything sounded peaceful. We drifted into a conversation about Alex and the situation with his parents.

"Alex knew they weren't getting along," Robert said. "He says he doesn't remember *when* they were happy together."

Jamie came wandering down from his second-floor bedroom, holding a paperback copy of *In the Night Kitchen*. I smiled and whispered, "Just a second, okay?"

He nodded and shuffled back upstairs.

". . . one night," Robert was saying, "oh, must have been about two or three in the morning, Alex heard a crashing noise and figured it was in his dream. The next morning his dad was gone and there was no toaster oven in the kitchen."

"Had he *thrown* it the night before?" I asked.

"Smashed it on the floor," Robert replied.

"Stacey," Jamie said, tiptoeing back into the kitchen, "my tummy hurts."

"Excuse me, Robert," I said. Then I turned to Jamie. "Well, sure it does. You haven't eaten all day."

Jamie looked cross. "But I'm not hungry!"

"Well, get yourself a drink of water, okay, big guy?"

Without answering, he clomped up the stairs again.

"Listen, Robert," I said into the phone. "I should go put Jamie to bed. But I want to hear all the details. I'll call you back."

"You bet."

I hung up and went upstairs. Jamie was in the bathroom, staring at the sink.

"I see a tired little boy," I said.

"I'm not little!"

"Which one's your toothbrush?" I asked.

"The blue one," he said, grabbing it off a rack. "And I can do it myself."

I patiently waited for him to brush. Then I patiently escorted him to bed, tucked him in, and read him *In the Night Kitchen*. "Good night, Jamie," I said afterward, rumpling his hair.

Jamie made a face.

"Are you okay?" I asked.

He yawned. "I feel yucky."

"Well, it's very late. You need a good

sleep." I stood up. "Sweet dreams."

" 'Night," he mumbled.

I raced back to the kitchen and called Robert.

"Acme Gossip Service," he answered.

"Okay," I said. "Go ahead."

"Well, everything was fine at Alex's house for the next two days. Mr. Zacharias said the toaster oven had blown a heating coil, but that was a lie. One night Alex couldn't sleep and went downstairs. His dad was zonked out on the living room couch."

"No!"

"Yes. And all his shaving stuff was in the downstairs bathroom."

"Stacey?" piped Jamie's voice from upstairs.

"Hold it, Robert." I called out, "What is it, Jamie?"

"Can you buzza brizz rammram."

I could not understand his mumbling at all. "Go to sleep, okay? It's late!"

Silence.

Well, Robert went on and on about the Zachariases. To sum it up, Alex's dad moved out and Alex was feeling devastated. He told Robert that his friendship with us meant a lot to him.

"WwwwaaaaAAA*AAAHHHH*!"

Jamie's latest cry was like a siren.

"Sorry, Robert, I don't know what's gotten into Jamie. I have to go."

"Okay. 'Bye."

" 'Bye!"

I hung up and trudged toward the stairs. "Jamie, what's the —"

I didn't bother to say *matter*. I didn't have to. I knew the answer before I even set foot on the stairs. The smell gave it away.

Now, I'm a pretty agreeable person. I don't hate many things in the world. But there's one thing I absolutely cannot stand.

Puke.

Even saying it — even thinking it — makes me feel sick.

"Wwwaaaaa-haaah-haaaa!"

There was no turning back now. Jamie was hysterical. I was his baby-sitter. And like it or not, I had to enter the land of El Barfo Grosso.

I ran into the living room, took a deep breath of fresh air, held it, ran back, and climbed the stairs.

Jamie was in the bathroom. He had thrown up in his bedroom. It didn't take a detective to figure that out. Between the two places, all down the hallway, was a long . . . trail.

Well, I refuse to go into any further gory details, except to say that (1) I did not pass out, (2) Jamie's bedroom carpet will either have to be replaced or dyed orange, and (3) I will never, ever eat macaroni and cheese again.

Poor Jamie. He was covered. He was also utterly, totally miserable.

I ran the bath. "Don't worry," I said. "You just wash yourself off and lie down."

"I *called* you and *called* you," Jamie blubbered, wiping the tears from his cheeks, "and you didn't come!"

"Ohhh, I'm sorry, Jamie."

What could I say? He was right. I felt awful.

As he began to peel off his pajamas, I ran downstairs to find cleaning supplies.

Okay, I will say it now. The next few minutes were the worst of my entire life. Bar none. If I deserved punishment for my phone conversation with Robert, I got it.

I scrubbed every crack in the wood hallway floor. I sponged every fiber of carpet. I used disinfectants and deodorizers I didn't even know existed. I changed Jamie's sheets. I found him a clean pair of pj's and sat with him while he had another "twinge."

I practically had to carry him to bed, he was so weak. The moment he hit the sheets, his eyes closed.

"Good night, Jamie," I said to his little, tear-streaked, sleepy face.

"Why didn't you come to me, Stacey?" were his last words before he nodded off.

I almost started crying. Boy, did I feel terrible. I'd let Jamie down when he needed me. Some baby-sitter.

The least I could do was leave the house spotless. I looked around. The floors seemed pretty clean. I might be able to run a wash before the Newtons arrived.

But you know barf smell. It has a way of saying, "Here I am!" when you least expect it. For days.

I took the yucky sheets and clothes to the basement and started the wash anyway. The Newtons arrived half an hour later. "Uh-oh," was the first thing Mr. Newton said. "Somebody had an accident."

"I'm so sorry," I said. "Jamie told me his tummy hurt, but I didn't take him seriously enough."

Mrs. Newton looked worried. "No wonder he didn't eat anything today. The poor thing must have a stomach virus."

"Stomach virus?" I said. "Oh, no. I forced him to eat his macaroni and cheese."

"You didn't know, Stacey," Mrs. Newton reassured me.

"We called you from the restaurant, Stacey," Mr. Newton said. "But the phone was busy."

Uh-oh. So much for Call Waiting.

"Yeah." I looked at the floor. "I was on the phone."

"For half an hour?" Mr. Newton asked. "We tried twice."

I nodded. "I shouldn't have gotten so carried away. It was wrong. I'll . . . I'll never do it again."

"Okay, Stacey, apology accepted," Mrs. Newton said gently.

I'm surprised she didn't bite my head off.

I could not believe how nice the Newtons were. I must have said, "I'm sorry," a hundred times. But they kept assuring me they weren't angry. They even thanked me for cleaning up and apologized that I had to put up with such a mess.

I smiled, thanked *them*, and left. But I felt rotten. And not only about Jamie.

First of all, I hadn't told the whole truth. I hadn't mentioned that I was yacking with a boyfriend.

Second of all, I knew Kristy was going to hear about this. She would figure out who I was talking to.

And she would not be so forgiving.

CHAPTER 11

"Hey, Claudia, that looks *great*!" Logan Bruno said.

As an associate member, Logan doesn't come to many BSC meetings. I was kind of glad he was at Wednesday's. Everyone tends to be on best behavior when he's around.

They were all gathered around a large, pink sheet of oaktag on Claudia's desk.

I slipped quietly in, dropped my coat on the floor, and tiptoed to the desk.

I caught a glimpse of Claudia's clock: five thirty-three.

Arrggghh. I'd been at Robert's house, too long as usual, jabbering about where to put the speakers and the food for the party.

No one seemed to notice my arrival. Maybe if I just acted normal . . .

"Well?" a sharp, accusing voice said to me.

I'll give you one guess who it was.

"Looks great," I said to Kristy, gesturing

toward the paper on Claud's desk. This is what it looked like:

THE FIRST ANNUAL
STONEYBROOK KIDS' TALENT SHOW!
MAGIC! COMEDY! MUSIC!
AND SURPRISES GALORE!

SPONSORED BY THE BABY-SITTERS CLUB
SATURDAY, 11:00 TO 12 NOON
BRING THE WHOLE FAMILY!

"Thanks," Claudia replied, looking up. "Mal was my spelling consultant."

Kristy was not going to be distracted from her quest. "Late again?" she said.

"Sorry," I replied. "I got carried away with a project."

Everyone was settling into place now. No one looked too happy.

"You know, nobody else has trouble getting here on time," Kristy said.

"I know," I replied. "I'll try. Really. I'll get back on track."

Kristy let out a big sigh. "We got a call from Mrs. Newton, Stacey."

Gulp. Dead silence.

I bowed my head. "I guess I blew it."

"She told us Jamie barfed," Kristy went on, "and you did a good cleanup job."

"Thanks." Could it be she didn't mention . . . ?

"And she made a special request that I tell all members to limit phone calls to emergencies."

Uh-oh. "Okay. I'm sorry."

"It was Robert, wasn't it?" Kristy pressed.

I nodded.

"You have to watch it, Stace," Logan said. "Remember what happened with Mary Anne and me at the Kuhns'."

I did remember. When Mary Anne was sitting for the Kuhn kids, she invited Logan over to play with Jake Kuhn, who was mopey because his dad had moved far away. When Mrs. Kuhn found out, she thought Mary Anne was having a boyfriend over behind her back.

"Well, this is a little different," I said. "I mean, Robert didn't come over."

"Still, Stacey," Dawn said, "you know you shouldn't have done it."

"I know." I folded my arms and looked away. Did they think I was proud of what I had done? Did they realize how much work it was to clean that stuff up? Didn't that count for *something*?

"We need to be able to rely on you, Stacey."
I don't know how Kristy manages it, but sometimes she sounds like a forty-year-old.

"I *know*!" I repeated. Tears were welling up in my eyes now. "It . . . it was a mistake!"

Claudia quickly spoke up. "Uh, what do you think, guys? Should I make copies of the flier?"

"I love it," Mallory told her.

"Me, too," Mary Anne agreed.

"Me, tutti frutti," Jessi piped up.

(Gag me.)

"Dad and Sharon say it's okay to use the barn," Mary Anne announced.

"Great," Kristy said. "What supplies will we need?"

"A boom box for music," Mallory volunteered. "I can bring that."

"Can we string up a curtain?" Claudia asked.

"Sure," Dawn replied. "Who wants to help?"

"Ooh! Ooh! Ooh!"

I couldn't believe it. They were all *raising their hands*. As if we were in school.

"How about an electrical outlet?" Mallory asked.

"We can run an extension cord from the house," Dawn suggested.

"I think we should provide refreshments,"

Kristy said. "The kids'll get hungry and thirsty."

"What about admission?" Jessi asked.

They talked about the show for the rest of the half hour, in between calls.

To tell you the truth, I didn't pay much attention. The talent show was not the top thing on my mind.

I had a nice, quiet dinner with Mom when I got home. The phone rang as we were finishing up.

Mom answered it and handed the receiver to me. "It's Char."

"Hi!" I said.

"Stacey, I'm scared," was Charlotte's greeting.

"What happened?" I asked.

"Nothing. It's just . . . you know . . . my piano playing."

"Oh, you're scared about the recital."

"No. The show. It's Saturday."

"Oh, Char, don't worry —"

"If I even *think* about it when I'm playing, I start making mistakes!"

"Charlotte, you're going to be great. You've made so much progress. I have total faith in you."

"You do?"

"Of course!"

"Really?"

"Really."

Charlotte sighed. "Okay."

"You feel better?"

"A little."

Boop! went our Call Waiting.

"Char, someone's trying to call us. I have to go."

"Okay. 'Bye."

" 'Bye."

I clicked the receiver hook. "Hello?"

"Hi, Stace," said Robert's voice. "I have bad news."

I sat down hard. "Uh-oh. Something about Alex?"

"No. He's fine. It's about the party. Um, can we have it at your house?"

"What happened?"

"Well, remember when you asked if I'd asked my parents about it?"

"Yeah."

"Well, I just did."

"Just now?"

"Mm-hm. And they said they had already invited some of their friends over Friday night."

"Oh."

I was not going to scold Robert. My own

life was full of too much scolding as it was. This was not the end of the world. We could work it out.

"Just a minute, Robert."

I ran into the living room, where my mom was sitting with a cup of coffee and a newspaper. "Mom, I know this is short notice, but Robert kind of messed up his party plans and wants to know if we could have it here on Friday?"

Mom dropped her paper. "The day after tomorrow?"

"Yeah."

She burst out laughing. "Well, if you do the planning and the cleanup, and all I have to do is look motherly, fine."

"Thanks, Mom!" I gave her a huge kiss on the cheek. "I love you!"

I ran back to the phone. "She says yes!" I told Robert.

He let out a whoop that almost broke my eardrum. I finished up the conversation using the other ear.

I was elated as I started doing the dishes. But that feeling didn't last long.

The more I thought the party through, the more the idea bothered me.

How on earth was I going to keep a party at my house a secret from the BSC? The noise would reach Mallory's, for sure. And even if it didn't, what if Dawn or Mary Anne called in the middle of it?

And even if none of those things happened, kids were going to talk about it at school. A party at Robert's was explainable, at least; he doesn't know the BSC members that well, so it would make sense he wouldn't invite them.

But this was a different story. And boy, did I feel guilty.

I flicked on the dishwasher and plopped onto a chair.

What a mess this was. Maybe I *should* invite my friends from the BSC, I thought, or at least make it up to them somehow — have another party for them, or organize a trip.

The phone rang then.

"Hello," I said, picking up the receiver.

"Hey, Stace," Claudia said. "What's up?"

I laughed. "I'm glad *someone* in the BSC is still talking to me."

"Yeah. Kristy really took her grouch pills today, huh?"

"Claudia, I have some weird news. The party plans changed. It has to be at my house."

"Whaaaat? I guess that means you have to invite the rest of the club, huh?"

"Well, I don't really want to."

"Ugh. This is weird."

"You'll still come, won't you?"

Claudia let out a deep breath. "I feel kind of funny, Stace. I mean, what am I going to say if someone finds out? They'll hate me, even though I really didn't do anything. I'm caught in the middle."

"Yeah," I said. "I can see what you mean."

"Think about it, okay?"

"Okay."

But I had made up my mind even before we said good-bye. I didn't want to ruin the party. I was going to go ahead with it.

I just hoped I wouldn't be caught.

CHAPTER 12

"Hello, I'm Stacey's mother."

BRRRRRRRRRR.

"Hi, Maureen McGill."

BRRRRRRRRRR.

"Hey, what's up? I'm the mom."

I walked into the kitchen. Mom was talking to a blender full of fresh fruit punch, pressing the MIX button every few seconds.

"Uh, excuse me," I said. "Are you feeling all right?"

"Yup," Mom replied. "Just trying to figure out the best way to introduce myself. Should I use the hip or formal approach?"

"Experiment," I said, trying not to laugh too hard.

BRRRRRRRRRR went the blender.

I looked at the kitchen clock: six forty-five. Fifteen minutes to party time!

Yes, Friday had arrived. The McGill house

was now Party Central. Already I was exhausted.

You have no idea how hard it was to keep the party a secret. All day at school, people were shouting, "See you tonight!" or asking for details. I carefully stayed away from my BSC friends. I ate lunch with Robert at the opposite end of the cafeteria.

I know, I know, it was sneaky. But it was better than having to explain the situation.

Robert and I met right after school. Together we did some last-minute shopping at the supermarket, then went straight to my house and neatened up. Mom came home from work early and helped out.

I kept my eye on the clock. No way was I going to be late for the BSC meeting that evening. The last thing I needed was another argument.

I kind of went overboard. It was five-fifteen when I arrived. Only Claudia was there.

"Oh, no!" she said, collapsing on the bed with shock. "Did you break up with Robert?"

"No," I replied, laughing.

"Were we supposed to set our clocks forward last night?"

"No! Why?"

"Why else would you be early?"

"Ha ha." I shut her bedroom door and lowered my voice. "Everything's almost set for the party. Can you bring some extra munchies — you know, whatever you have lying around here?"

"Sure. Can I borrow a wheelbarrow?"

"Just whatever you can hold."

Claudia's face grew serious. "Um, Stacey, I don't know how to say this, but I've been having second thoughts about coming to the party."

"You *have* to come!" I insisted. "What happened? Did someone find out about it?"

"I'm not sure. After school, Dawn was asking me these questions —"

We couldn't finish the conversation. The door creaked open and in walked Kristy. She, of course, made a big show of being surprised to see me. (Somehow, when *she* did it, it wasn't as funny.)

The meeting was super-busy that day. We didn't do much besides answer the phone. Dawn seemed quiet, but she didn't ask any questions. No one did.

I was a little nervous, but mostly I couldn't wait to leave. I was practically sick with excitement.

At precisely six o'clock I raced home. Robert was still setting up. "I think we need more chips," he suggested.

That was when I dashed into the kitchen and caught Mom introducing herself to the blender.

I ate a snack, then grabbed some bags of chips and pretzels from the cupboard and went back to the living room to help.

At 7:07, the doorbell rang.

Robert and I both ran to open the door.

It was Alex and Andi. "Heyyyy, what's up?" Alex said, holding out a shopping bag to us. "We brought sugarless cookies."

"Thanks," I said. (Now, how many friends would be *that* thoughtful?)

"Hi," Mom said, walking into the living room with a big smile, "I'm Stacey's mother."

Now she was wearing a baseball cap with the bill turned to the back. (She chose formal words and casual dress, I guess.) Fortunately, she was not carrying the blender. I gave her a thumbs-up sign as she shook hands with my friends.

Alex and Andi gave Mom their coats. Robert put on some music.

And then the rush began.

One by one, cars pulled up to the front and parents dropped off their kids. Wayne and Sheila came with a gorgeous bouquet of flowers. Claudia brought two shopping bags full of junk food. (Some of it was Halloween candy. Lord knows where she found that.)

She also brought what looked like a painting, all wrapped up in brown paper. "What's that?" I asked.

Claudia was grinning. "A present. Open it."

I tore open the paper and gasped.

It was *Anastasia Fantasia* — Claudia's abstract portrait of me. A tag was taped to it that said *To my friend forever. Love, Claudia.*

"Oh, Claudia, thank you!" I gave her a big hug and whispered, "And thanks for coming, too."

I brought the painting into the living room to a chorus of oohs and aahs. Then I put it on the fireplace mantel, where everyone could admire it.

Before long the house was jammed. I put on one of my dance CDs, and — surprise, surprise — everybody danced! (Well, *you* know, it doesn't always work that way.)

Mom bustled around, moving breakable objects far from the flailing arms. Then she started dancing, too, baseball cap and all.

You know what? She didn't look too dorky. In fact, a lot of the guys danced with her (including Robert, of course).

When Mom brought out her homemade, blender-mixed fruit punch, she became even more popular.

Everywhere I looked, kids were laughing and having a great time. No one was being shy. Boys and girls were mixing. Some had paired off. I caught a glimpse of a kiss here and there.

Before that day, I hadn't even known a lot of these kids. They were all coming up to me and saying what a great party it was.

I could not stop smiling. I thought my cheeks would crack. This was definitely, absolutely THE coolest party I had ever been to.

When the doorbell rang at about nine o'clock, I didn't hear it at first. I was in the middle of a dance with Robert. My hair was flying in front of my face. I was singing along with the song.

Claudia tapped me on the shoulder. "Stacey, I think —"

Ding-dong!

I heard that one. I flung open the door in mid-dance.

Then I froze.

Standing there, bundled up in down coats, were Dawn and Mary Anne.

"Hi, Stacey," Dawn said flatly. "Looks like you're busy."

"Uh, hi." I pushed my hair away from my face. Without thinking, I pulled the door partway closed behind me.

Dawn was smirking. Mary Anne's eyes were brimming with tears.

I gulped. Words formed in my brain, but I couldn't get them out.

Finally an "Urrgh" squeezed out of my throat. (Real smooth.) I swallowed and tried again. "Uh, want to come in?"

"No, that's okay," Dawn said. "We thought we'd stop by, since you hadn't mentioned you were doing anything. I guess you just forgot, huh?"

I felt the door yanking open behind me. "Stace," Claudia's voice called out, "is everything —"

The smugness drained from Dawn's face.

Mary Anne's jaw fell open. "Claudia?" she said.

"Oh. Um, hi," Claudia mumbled. "Welcome to the party."

Dawn shook her head. "No, Claud. It looks like some of us aren't."

With that, they turned around and left.

Claudia and I stood there like twin marble statues. We watched Mary Anne and Dawn disappear down Elm Street.

"Uh-oh," Claudia said under her breath.

We moved inside and I shut the door. Claudia's face was pale. Her eyes were welling up.

"They must all know about it," I said.

"Well, of course they do," Claudia snapped. "Half our classmates were invited to this party. Did you really expect them not to find out?"

"Sorry, Claudia."

"Yeah."

"Look, it was a hard decision. I didn't mean to —"

"Why did you drag me into this, Stacey?" Claudia blurted out. "Why didn't you listen when I tried to back out of this party? I thought we were friends forever. Friends don't do this kind of thing to one another. I wish . . . I wish you'd never met *Robert*."

She practically spat his name out, then turned and stomped toward the kitchen.

Oh, no.

I slumped against the wall. I couldn't believe this. I thought about a fight Claud and I had had last summer. I had invited her to Fire Island without telling her that Robert was going to be there. She was hurt and angry, but we managed to patch that one up. I had hoped we'd never have such a bad misunderstanding again.

And now this happened.

Two strikes, McGill, I said to myself.

I wondered if I'd get a third.

The party continued until eleven o'clock or so. I mingled. I danced. I ate. But my heart wasn't in it.

After everyone left, I told Robert what had happened. He tried to comfort me. He even volunteered to talk to my friends himself.

I said no. They'd probably throw him out the window.

I said we'd be better off convincing our parents to move far, far away.

The moon might be nice.

CHAPTER 13

Saterday
~~Today~~ was the big talant show. The
event of the weak. It was so ~~exit~~ ~~was~~
~~exit~~ thriling. What a perfict, happy,
carefree day. . . .

Claudia was exaggerating. I think she was trying to make everybody feel better about the disaster the night before.

I was a wreck that morning. I had spent half the night feeling guilty, the other half feeling furious. Neither was exactly the perfect mood for sleep.

Anyway, I overslept. And when I finally woke up, all I could think about was how I had blown it. How could I possibly face Dawn or Mary Anne or Claudia at the talent show?

I couldn't. I decided to stay home.

I found out the details from Claudia, eventually. (It was a long, long time before she would speak to me like a human being.)

Friday night, Claud had left my party early. She felt so terrible, she walked straight over to Dawn's and Mary Anne's to apologize.

I guess they forgave her, because the three of them sat down and made a huge banner to hang across the barn door. It read: *This is the place! Kid's talant show! 11:00!*

Saturday morning, as they were putting up the banner, Maria Kilbourne showed up.

"What's tal-*ant*?" she said.

Dawn and Mary Anne looked at the banner and groaned. "Why didn't we see that?" Mary Anne asked.

Claudia, as you may have noticed, is the

111

world's worst speller. She ran out of the barn, where she'd been hanging a curtain. "Is it *int*?" she asked.

"*Ent*," Mary Anne replied. "I'll get a marker and change it."

"Where's your boom box?" Maria asked.

"I'll get that, too," Mary Anne replied. "And the extension cord."

Maria walked into the barn and gasped. "Oh, no! It's dirt."

"What?" Claudia said.

"The floor!" Maria answered. "How can I tap on dirt?"

"Well, it's . . . *hard* dirt," Claudia offered. "Sort of like cement."

"Cement is bad for your hamstrings."

"Kristy's basement floor was cement covered with tiles. You tapped there."

"Oh."

WWWAAAAANNNNNK!

Claudia jumped. Byron had sneaked up behind her and blown his harmonica into her ear.

"Thanks a lot!" Claudia said.

Laughing, Byron ran into the barn, followed by the rest of the Pike tribe.

Next the Papadakises showed up. Linny proudly showed off a Greek fisherman's cap with a plastic bottle sewn to the top. "For the bottle dance," he explained.

The next fifteen minutes or so were pure chaos, as kids, parents, and baby-sitters began to arrive. The BSC hadn't limited the number of performers, which was looking like a big mistake. When Mary Anne brought out her boom box, she was mobbed by kids waving cassettes.

Things went downhill from there. Maria insisted every last bit of straw be swept off the floor. David Michael dropped his Daffy Duck puppet into an oil slick near the lawn mower and had to borrow a Porky Pig that Mary Anne had stashed away. Jordan whacked Jessi in the face by accident when she was trying to give him dance pointers. Charlotte informed Claudia that the apostrophe was in the wrong place on the poster. (It should have been KIDS', not KID'S.)

Between the cleaning, the dancing, the singing, the setting up of chairs, and the banner corrections, Claudia thought the show would never get off the ground.

Then, just as things were quieting down, Dawn handed out a neatly typed Order of Ceremonies.

"I'm *fifth*? No fair!" Buddy Barrett shouted.

Everyone started complaining at once. Linny and Buddy started a shoving match.

And that was when Kristy arrived.

PHWEEEEET!

Kristy loves to blow her referee's whistle. Especially indoors. She shouldn't. It causes hearing damage. All dogs within a five-mile radius start howling.

The barn, needless to say, fell silent.

"Okay," Kristy announced. "We'll use this order of ceremonies, unless someone has a medical excuse." (Medical excuse? I don't know how she thought of that one.) "I will now shut the curtain and we will begin seating our guests. In precisely fifteen minutes the show will begin. I will announce each performer when his or her time comes. At intermission I will ask for volunteers to help with refreshments. Is that understood?"

A barnful of little heads nodded yes.

"And have fun!" Claudia added. (Well, someone had to say it. The kids must have thought they'd wandered into boot camp by mistake.)

I have to hand it to Kristy. She'd calmed things down. The kids had become angels. Dawn led them to the back of the barn and sat them on chairs. Mallory gave them a brief pep talk.

Logan and Mary Anne stood ready to open the curtain, which was actually two sheets hung on a rod suspended by ropes.

"It's a full house!" Mary Anne called out to the cast and crew.

"Okay, let's go!" Kristy whispered.

Logan yanked his half of the curtain dramatically, pulling the rod toward him. That caused Mary Anne to let go of her half, which fell across Kristy's face as she stepped forward.

"Sorry!" Mary Anne cried out.

"Harrumph," Kristy said, untangling herself. "Ladies and gentlemen and children of all ages, on behalf of the Baby-sitters Club, who will be happy to assist all parents in their child care needs; just ask a member at intermission if you're unfamiliar with —"

"Pssst! Go on!" Logan urged her.

"Um, I welcome you to our first annual talent show!"

Thunderous applause.

"It's my pleasure to present, with a treacherous dance of balance and skill . . . Linny Papadakis!"

Riotous applause.

Linny strutted onto the stage and took a bow. The problem was, the Greek hat was too big and floppy. Since the bottle was glued to it, they both fell off.

And they continued to do so throughout the treacherous bottle dance.

That didn't stop Linny. He finished the dance with one hand firmly holding the hat on his head.

Next, Buddy did his famous imitations —

Bugs Bunny, Sylvester the Cat, Yogi Bear, and Mickey Mouse.

Each of which sounded remarkably like Buddy Barrett.

Then Maria stepped out and said, "Um, I'm going to tap now, but it's dirt so you have to imagine the taps being louder."

The audience *loved* her.

Adam did some magic tricks with linking rings, then tried to pull a quarter out of Sari Papadakis's ear. She ran off, wailing, and refused to come back to sing "Twinkle, Twinkle, Little Star."

So Emily Michelle had to do a solo, and that brought down the house.

Which caused Linny to stand up and yell, "No fair! Rematch!"

Hannie sang in a little, quavery voice and forgot most of her song. By the second verse she just sang the words "Sunrise, Sunset" over and over again to the tune. Everyone clapped anyway, which made her beam with pride. (Later she told her parents, "I sang so beautifully, no one even knew I made a mistake!")

Bill and Melody sang "A Whole New World" holding hands. Claudia said some grownups (and Mary Anne) were crying.

Claudia's favorite part was watching Claire

Pike dance with veils to the music of Byron's harmonica and Adam's spoons.

Toward the end of the program, Kristy launched into a long intro while Mallory helped Charlotte set up her electric piano. "And now, a special treat for you all. Charlotte Johanssen, who has been studying piano intensively for weeks, shall play a song by the famous composer . . . um, by one of the great musicians of all time . . ."

Kristy glanced back toward Charlotte.

That was when Claudia noticed that Charlotte was looking into the audience. Her face was ashen.

"By . . . by . . ." Kristy sputtered.

"Nobody," Mallory whispered. "It's just a *song*."

"Song . . . heim. Stephen Songheim!" Kristy improvised. "And now, without further ado, let's give it up for Charlotte Johanssen."

The audience burst into applause.

Charlotte stared. Her eyes darted left and right. "Um . . . um . . ."

"It's all right, go ahead," Mallory urged her.

"Um . . ." Charlotte repeated. And then, in a meek voice, she called out, "*Stacey?*"

People in the audience began turning around to look for me. Someone else called out, "Is Stacey McGill here?"

Oh, my heart. It is still painful even to think about what happened next.

When no one answered, Charlotte's lips began to quiver. Her knees shook. In the back of the crowd, Dr. Johanssen stood up and held out her arms.

Charlotte raced off the stage to her mom, sobbing.

As Kristy nervously introduced the next act, the Johanssens tiptoed out of the barn.

Claudia ran after them. "Charlotte? Are you all right?" she called out.

"Wh — wh — where's Stacey?" Char asked between sobs.

"I don't know," Claudia replied. "Maybe she had a doctor's appointment or something."

"She can't have a doctor's appointment! She promised she'd be here!" Charlotte cried. *"Promised!"*

The Johanssens both hugged her tighter.

"I'm sorry, Char," Claudia said.

Charlotte reached into a pocket and pulled out a neatly folded piece of paper. "I . . . I had a s-speech all planned, too."

Claudia unfolded the paper and read:

I would like to dedicate this song to my friend and almost-sister, Stacey McGill.

Claudia got all choked up reading that. And

118

not only because it was so touching or sweet or genuine.

She was angry. Fuming. She knew why I hadn't shown up. She knew I wanted to avoid the BSC. She just couldn't believe I'd let Charlotte down for such a petty reason.

(It wasn't petty to *me*, though. It was a real crisis. But I couldn't believe I'd let it hurt Charlotte.)

"Don't worry, Char," Claudia said softly. "I'll talk to her. I know she'll apologize to you."

As the Johanssens left, Claudia went back in the barn and watched the rest of the show.

She stayed to help clean up afterward. Kristy and Dawn commented on my absence, but only briefly. Everyone was too busy talking about the show.

The minute Claudia got home, she called me.

"Stacey McGill, you better have a good reason for not showing up today," was the first thing she said. "You totally destroyed Charlotte Johanssen."

I felt suddenly faint when I realized what I'd done. "Oh, my lord."

"Mm-hm, that's right, you blew it, Stacey," Claud barged on. "You blew it last night and you blew it this morning. What is it? Do you *want* everybody to hate you?"

"N-no!" I stammered. "I just — I just —"

"You just better show up to the club meeting on Monday. On time. That's all I can say."

And it *was* all she said.

Claudia Kishi, my ex-best friend, hung up on me.

CHAPTER 14

I went over to Charlotte's Saturday evening. She was cold to me at first, but I explained to her what had happened. The truth. Char is only eight, but she listened and absorbed it all. She could understand the emotions I was going through.

I only wish *I* could.

Don't ask me what I did Saturday night or Sunday. I vaguely remember talking to Robert on the phone, but that's about it. I pretty much kept to myself. I must have been in shock.

Monday morning was warm and springlike, but I barely noticed. By the time I reached school, I was shaking. I felt as if my entire world had warped and twisted, like a funhouse mirror. Nothing was the same as it had been a month ago. A week ago.

Back then, I would have begged forgiveness from my friends in the BSC. I would have tried like crazy to balance my time between school, the club, Robert, and my family. I would have gone on feeling guilty about my boyfriend at BSC meetings, embarrassed about one set of friends while I was with the other.

But I wasn't feeling apologetic now. Or guilty. Or ashamed.

The strange thing was, I didn't know *how* to feel. I was going to have to figure that out.

I saw Kristy between homeroom and first period, but I walked the other way. I made sure to avoid Claudia, Dawn, and Mary Anne (which wasn't hard; I think they were doing the same with me). During lunch I went to the library. I walked home partway with Robert, but we each split off to go to our own houses.

I did, however, arrive at the BSC meeting on time. I made sure of that.

No one said hello to me when I walked in. But I kind of expected that. Claudia offered pretzels, but Kristy was the only taker.

At precisely five-thirty, as usual, Kristy said, "I hereby call the Monday meeting of the Baby-sitters Club to order."

"It's dues day," I announced.

Everyone handed over dues solemnly, without a single complaint.

"Any new business?" Kristy asked.

Click, went Claudia's clock.

I've heard that in the moments before an

earthquake, all nature falls completely silent. Birds alight and stop chirping, squirrels stop running, rivers stop flowing.

I don't know if this is true or not, but that's what the meeting felt like at that moment. An eerie, unnatural quiet before something awful.

Claudia finally let out a big sigh. "Okay, if no one's going to say it, I will. Stacey, we have only a half hour. You had better start explaining yourself now."

I laughed. I don't know why, I just did. "Sure. Any specific questions?"

Kristy exploded. "Listen to you! How can you be so . . . so . . ."

"Callous," Dawn supplied.

"Callous!" Kristy said. "After everything you've done! What's happened to you, Stacey? Ever since you met Robert —"

"Kristy," I said, "would you please leave Robert out of this?"

"Uh-uh, no way, Stacey," Mallory cut in (yes, meek little Mallory). "You weren't like this before you met him."

"Like what?" I shot back. "Like a person who wants to have a life outside the Baby-sitters Club? Like someone who goes out with other friends from time to time? You're all like that, somewhere inside. Maybe you need to grow up and find out —"

"*Grow up*?" Dawn snapped. "Look who's talking about growing up!"

"Okay, whoa, chill!" Claudia said. "Look, this is my room and I don't want a shouting match. Stacey, I think it's fair to say that everyone's wondering about you. I mean, boyfriends are cool. Nobody disagrees. So you were late to a few meetings, big deal. That's not the point. But let's face it, you got carried away at the Newtons', and look what happened."

"I know," I said. "That was a mistake, and I learned from it. Okay?"

"But," Mary Anne piped up, then stopped herself. "Oh, nothing."

"Go on, Mary Anne," Kristy insisted.

"Well, all I want to do is ask a question." It was painful to see Mary Anne speak up. She hates confrontation. "You know, about the party, Stacey. Why didn't you invite us? I mean, we *are* your friends, aren't we?"

"Look," I said patiently, "Robert has his circle of friends. I have mine. Parts of our circles intersect, like Venn diagrams." (Oops, math. I could see Claudia's eyes glaze over.) "Anyway, some parts don't. The party was a spur-of-the-moment thing for the kids Robert and I hang out with together. That's all. Is that such a big deal? I don't invite *them* to every BSC event, do I? They don't get insulted. Be-

124

sides, the party was supposed to be at Robert's. We had to use my house at the last minute."

"I guess you have an explanation for everything," Kristy remarked.

"What's that supposed to mean?" I asked.

"Well," Kristy replied, "what I want to know is, how did Claudia end up in Robert's part of the Venn diagram, and the rest of us didn't?"

"Oh, Kristy, come on," I said.

"The least you could have done is not humiliate us," Dawn cut in. "The whole *school* knew about the party."

"If it bothered you so much, why didn't you have the maturity to call me?" I asked. "Instead of showing up at the party in front of all those people and saying 'Nyah-nyah' and spoiling everything."

"Maturity?" Kristy repeated. "Oh, please, Stacey. If you were so mature, why didn't *you* call Dawn and Mary Anne that night? Whether they were right or wrong, you knew their feelings were hurt."

"I didn't call them because I was angry!"

"So angry that you skipped out of the talent show the next day," Claudia continued. "So angry that you forgot about Charlotte Johanssen, who loves you so much and was counting on you. Real mature, Stace."

125

I knew someone would bring that up. "Look, I went over to Charlotte's on Saturday and apologized," I replied.

"Guess she kind of got lost on the old Venn diagram, too, huh?" Kristy remarked.

"Oh, Kristy, will you stop being such a stupid little baby?" I snapped.

"That's what this is all about, isn't it?" Kristy railroaded on. "We're all babies to you, aren't we? We embarrass you."

"Kris*tyyyy*," I warned.

"I notice you're not denying it," Kristy said. "Hey, I saw the look on your face that night at Burger Town."

"Kristy, you were putting straws up your nose and playing with your food and giggling out loud!"

"Oh, now we have to watch our behavior in public," Dawn said with a sneer. "We're not like mega-cool Stacey and her mega-cool friends."

That did it. I began seeing red. "At least I don't go spying behind jukeboxes and making an idiot out of myself by acting superior to waiters!"

"Stacey, stop it!" Claudia said. "If you can't discuss this —"

"This is not a discussion!" I replied. "This is a firing squad. I can't believe I'm sitting here and taking this. You don't want to be my friends. You want to control my life."

"That's the stupidest thing I ever heard," Kristy said.

"Yeah, well, anything *you* don't think of is stupid. I'm tired of your bossiness, Kristy. And that's not all. I'm sick of the meetings, week in and week out. And the rules. And the talent shows and fairs and contests and field trips and tantrums and stomach viruses and diapers and feeding schedules and sibling rivalries. I've had it! I'm thirteen years old! I want to spend time with kids who act my own age and talk about something besides baby-sitting."

Jessi, who had been silent all this time, said, "No one's forcing you to be here, Stacey."

"You're right." I stood up and grabbed my coat. "I quit the Baby-sitters Club!"

Kristy shot up out of the director's chair. "Oh, yeah? Well, you can't quit!"

"Why not?"

"Because you're fired!"

Fine with me. I turned, left, and didn't look back.

CHAPTER 15

"No, tilt it a little to the right," Alex said. "Yeah, that's it! Perfect."

I took a piece of tape from Robert, rolled it behind the Ferrari poster, and pressed down.

The interior decoration of Alex's new bedroom was complete.

It was a Monday, a week after the Big Explosion at the BSC meeting. I wasn't angry anymore. I tried not to think about it.

Alex and his mom had moved into a small house down the road from Robert. Alex felt kind of sad and kind of relieved, now that his parents' split was official (I sure knew *that* feeling). Robert, Andi, and I had gone over to his new house after school the past three days to help him move in.

"I like it," Alex said, surveying the room. "I think I'll stay."

"Anybody want a snack?" Mrs. Zacharias called from downstairs.

Robert, of course, was the first to answer. "Sure!"

Alex's mom had laid out cheese, crackers, and a bowl of fruit on the kitchen table.

"This cheese is great," Robert said, shoving a hunk of it into his mouth.

"It tastes nice with a cracker," Mrs. Zacharias gently hinted.

Robert raised his eyebrows, as if he had been told an interesting little tidbit about elegant dining. "Mm-hm."

I couldn't help but laugh. Lately I'd had a lot of time to get used to Robert's funny habits. The good ones and the bad ones.

I learned something after my big fight. For one thing, I had been right about some of the things I'd said. I'd been fitting my life in around the Baby-sitters Club. Take Robert, for instance. He had always seemed perfect to me, instead of like a normal human. That was why I so often felt nervous in front of him. Now I was seeing his sloppiness, his carelessness, his habit of talking with his mouth full. I was kind of glad. It meant I was seeing the real Robert.

My other friendships deepened, too. Alex needed a lot of moral support about life as a divorced kid, and I was able to be there for him. Andi and I turned out to have tons in common, and we had a few long phone conversations. We spent lots of time with Wayne and Sheila, hanging out after school.

My friends in the Baby-sitters Club? I missed them. Really. I mean, I'd had a lot of fun. I missed shopping and joking with Claudia, Mary Anne's kindness, Jessi's and Mallory's energy. I even missed Kristy's great ideas and Dawn's crusades. And the idea that I wouldn't be sitting much anymore really hurt. It had only been a week, but I missed seeing *kids*.

I hadn't talked to any of my friends since the fight. It was painful to pass a BSC member in the hallway at school and not say anything. I must have reached for the phone a thousand times to call Claudia, only to stop myself. Sometimes I felt like apologizing to everybody about the things I had said and done.

But only sometimes.

I guess the situation is still sinking in. It's hard to change your life so drastically. Friends aren't like clothes; you can't just discard them when you need a new wardrobe.

I was thinking about all of this when I realized it was already quarter after five. "Yikes," I said, "I'm going to be late!" I stood up. "See you guys later!"

" 'Bye!" everyone called out.

I headed up Elm Street, toward Bradford

Court. Out of the corner of my eye, I thought I saw Dawn Schafer walking toward Claudia's.

I kept going. A half a block down the road was a small stone church with a hand-drawn sign out front:

MRS. WOODS' BEGINNING STUDENTS
PIANO RECITAL
TODAY, 5:30 P.M.
CHURCH COMMON ROOM

Dr. and Mr. Johanssen were milling outside the door with some other parents. I said a quick hello as I darted inside.

The seats in the common room were almost all empty. Including the one front row, center.

I sat down in that one.

A baby grand piano stood in the space in front of me. Beyond it was a door that led to another room. I could see Charlotte in there, pacing nervously, all dressed up in a plaid skirt and ruffly white blouse.

When she glanced out the door, I gave her a thumbs-up sign.

She burst into a grin. Then she blushed and looked at her music.

People were starting to file in. To my left, muffled chimes rang out.

I turned to see an old mahogany grandfather clock. Its hands pointed to five-thirty.

Five-thirty on a Friday evening.

I felt a slight tug of sadness in my chest. Then I smiled and turned back to the piano.

The recital was about to begin.

About the Author

ANN M. MARTIN did *a lot* of baby-sitting when she was growing up in Princeton, New Jersey. She is a former editor of books for children, and was graduated from Smith College.

Ms. Martin lives in New York City with her cats, Mouse and Rosie. She likes ice cream and *I Love Lucy*; and she hates to cook.

Ann Martin's Apple Paperbacks include *Yours Turly, Shirley; Ten Kids, No Pets; With You and Without You; Bummer Summer*; and all the other books in the Baby-sitters Club series.

Look for #84

DAWN AND THE SCHOOL SPIRIT WAR

On the way home from school that day I thought Mary Anne was feeling better about things.

That night, though, after supper, I found her sitting in her room with the schedule of events on her lap. And she was crying! Real tears!

"Mary Anne," I cried, kneeling on the rug beside her chair. "What's the matter?"

"I can't go through with this pajama thing," she said, wiping her eyes. "But I don't want Logan to think I don't have school spirit. He's *so* into School Spirit Month. I feel like I'm being disloyal to him by not wanting to do this."

"Mary Anne, you're the most loyal person I've ever met," I said honestly. "Logan would never think that."

"Maybe not, but he'll be disappointed in me, even if he doesn't say so," Mary Anne insisted. "And all the other kids will think I'm a wimp, too."

"What do you care?"

"Well, I care what Claudia, Kristy, Mallory, and Jessi think."

"Don't worry about Mal," I said. "I don't think Pajama Day is her kind of thing, either."

"Maybe not, but the others will think I have no sense of humor or something." Mary Anne blinked back more tears. "Are you going to do it?"

"I don't know," I admitted. "I haven't been thinking about it like you have. I don't really want to."

"Then don't," said Mary Anne.

I thought about it a moment, and the more I thought the less I wanted to do it.

Read all the books
about **Stacey**
in the Baby-sitters Club series
by Ann M. Martin

THE BABY-SITTERS Club®

by Ann M. Martin

More titles... ▶

❑ MG45659-8	#58 Stacey's Choice	$3.50
❑ MG45660-1	#59 Mallory Hates Boys (and Gym)	$3.50
❑ MG45662-8	#60 Mary Anne's Makeover	$3.50
❑ MG45663-6	#61 Jessi's and the Awful Secret	$3.50
❑ MG45664-4	#62 Kristy and the Worst Kid Ever	$3.50
❑ MG45665-2	#63 Claudia's ~~Freind~~ Friend	$3.50
❑ MG45666-0	#64 Dawn's Family Feud	$3.50
❑ MG45667-9	#65 Stacey's Big Crush	$3.50
❑ MG47004-3	#66 Maid Mary Anne	$3.50
❑ MG47005-1	#67 Dawn's Big Move	$3.50
❑ MG47006-X	#68 Jessi and the Bad Baby-Sitter	$3.50
❑ MG47007-8	#69 Get Well Soon, Mallory!	$3.50
❑ MG47008-6	#70 Stacey and the Cheerleaders	$3.50
❑ MG47009-4	#71 Claudia and the Perfect Boy	$3.50
❑ MG47010-8	#72 Dawn and the We Love Kids Club	$3.50
❑ MG45575-3	Logan's Story Special Edition Readers' Request	$3.25
❑ MG47118-X	Logan Bruno, Boy Baby-sitter Special Edition Readers' Request	$3.50
❑ MG44240-6	Baby-sitters on Board! Super Special #1	$3.95
❑ MG44239-2	Baby-sitters' Summer Vacation Super Special #2	$3.95
❑ MG43973-1	Baby-sitters' Winter Vacation Super Special #3	$3.95
❑ MG42493-9	Baby-sitters' Island Adventure Super Special #4	$3.95
❑ MG43575-2	California Girls! Super Special #5	$3.95
❑ MG43576-0	New York, New York! Super Special #6	$3.95
❑ MG44963-X	Snowbound Super Special #7	$3.95
❑ MG44962-X	Baby-sitters at Shadow Lake Super Special #8	$3.95
❑ MG45661-X	Starring the Baby-sitters Club Super Special #9	$3.95
❑ MG45674-1	Sea City, Here We Come! Super Special #10	$3.95

Available wherever you buy books...or use this order form.

Scholastic Inc., P.O. Box 7502, 2931 E. McCarty Street, Jefferson City, MO 65102

Please send me the books I have checked above. I am enclosing $_____
(please add $2.00 to cover shipping and handling). Send check or money order - no cash or C.O.D.s please.

Name _____ Birthdate_____

Address _____

City_____ State/Zip _____

Please allow four to six weeks for delivery. Offer good in the U.S. only. Sorry, mail orders are not available to residents of Canada. Prices subject to change.

Create Your Own Mystery Stories!

MYSTERY GAME !

WHO: Boyfriend   **WHY:** Romance

WHAT: Phone Call   **WHERE:** Dance

Use the special Mystery Case card to pick WHO did it, WHAT was involved, WHY it happened and WHERE it happened. Then dial secret words on your Mystery Wheels to add to the story! Travel around the special Stoneybrook map gameboard to uncover your friends' secret word clues! Finish four baby-sitting jobs and find out all the words to win. Then have everyone join in to tell the story!